Facts about Paul:

- As a boy, Paul enjoyed birdwatching, which later inspired him to write the song "Blackbird."

- Paul met George Harrison on a bus to school when they were in their early teens.

- Paul was one of the first and last musicians to perform at Shea Stadium in New York. The Beatles performed there in August 1965, and 43 years later, on July 18, 2008, Paul performed "Let It Be," the closing number at Billy Joel's concert at Shea — the last concert before the stadium was torn down in 2009.

- Paul was only 16 years old when he wrote "When I'm 64." The song was released in 1966, the year his father, Jim, turned 64.

- In 2008, Paul was granted an honorary Doctorate of Music degree from Yale University.

- Paul is the tallest member of The Beatles — an inch shy of 6 feet.

- On the famous *Abbey Road* album cover, McCartney is barefoot.

- The 1982 song "Here Today" is about Paul's relationship with and love for John Lennon. Paul said the song is an imaginary conversation the two might have had.

Paul McCartney

Born: June 18, 1942

Marriages:
Linda Eastman, March 12, 1969-April 17,1998 (Linda's death from cancer)
Heather Mills, June 11, 2002-2008
Nancy Shevall, Oct. 9, 2011-present (wedding was on John's 71st birthday)

Children:
Heather McCartney, born Dec. 31, 1962 (adopted by Paul)
Mary McCartney, born Aug. 28, 1969
Stella McCartney, born Sept. 13, 1971
James McCartney, born Sept. 12, 1977
Beatrice McCartney, born Oct. 28, 2003

the Beatles

Our favorite Beatles' songs!

Editor Ben Nussbaum
You've Got to Hide Your Love Away

Chief Content Officer June Kikuchi
We Can Work It Out

Managing Editor Jennifer Taylor
All You Need is Love

Art Director Jerome Callens
While My Guitar Gently Weeps

Associate Art Director Terri Blake
P.S. I Love You

Contributing Editors Roger Sipe *Ticket to Ride*
Karen Julian *Lovely Rita*

Multimedia Production Coord. Leah Rosalez
In My Life

i-5 publishing

Chief Executive Officer Mark Harris
Michelle
Chief Financial Officer Nicole Fabian
Let It Be
Chief Sales Officer Jeff Scharf
Drive My Car
VP, Consumer Marketing Beth Freeman Reynolds
Hey Jude
Digital General Manager Melissa Kauffman
A Day in the Life
Book Division General Manager Christopher Reggio
Love Me Do
Marketing Director Lisa MacDonald
Eleanor Rigby
Multimedia Production Dir. Laurie Panaggio
She's Leaving Home
Controller Craig Wisda
Strawberry Fields Forever

Editorial, Production and Corporate Office
3 Burroughs, Irvine, CA 92618 ● 949-855-8822

The Toppermost of the Poppermost

AP PHOTO / HEINZ DUCKLAU

The year 1963 saw the Beatles take over the U.K. and lay the groundwork for Beatlemania in America.

BY IAN INGLIS

The only topic of conversation in Britain at the start of 1963 was the weather. Snow had started to fall in the last week of December and continued to do so for much of the next three months. January was the coldest month since 1814. Schools closed, lakes and rivers froze, transport networks came to a halt.

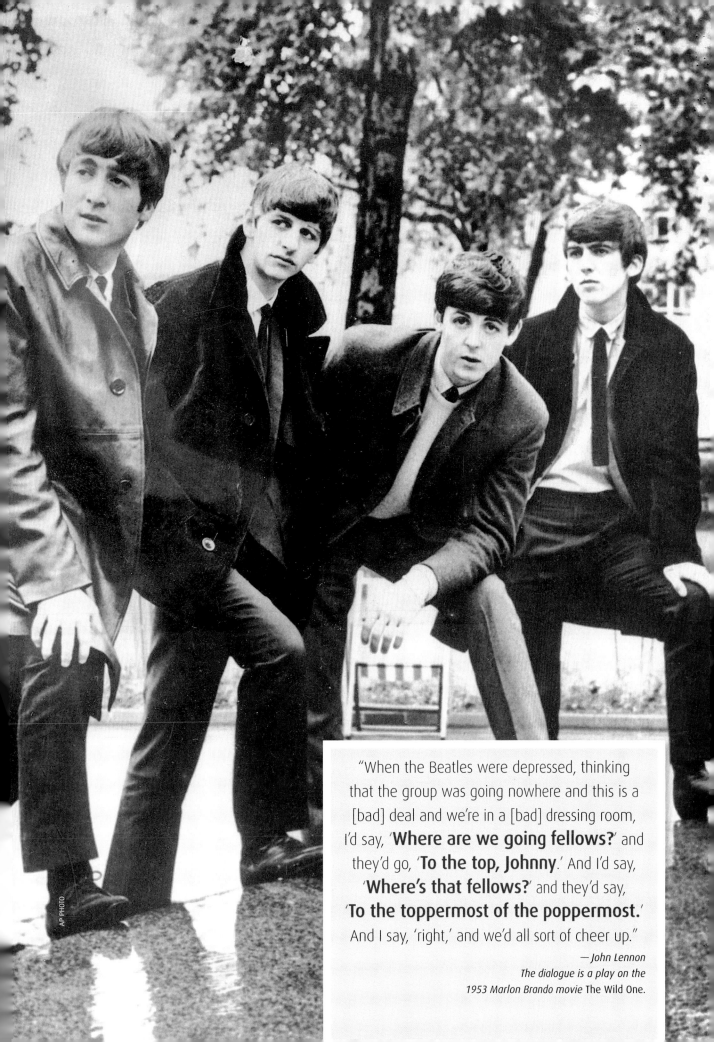

"When the Beatles were depressed, thinking that the group was going nowhere and this is a [bad] deal and we're in a [bad] dressing room, I'd say, **'Where are we going fellows?'** and they'd go, **'To the top, Johnny.'** And I'd say, **'Where's that fellows?'** and they'd say, **'To the toppermost of the poppermost.'** And I say, 'right,' and we'd all sort of cheer up."

— *John Lennon*
The dialogue is a play on the 1953 Marlon Brando movie The Wild One.

Another Year

When John Lennon, Paul McCartney, George Harrison and Ringo Starr flew into London on New Year's Day 1963 after completing a third and final season at Manfred Weissleder's Star-Club in Hamburg, they were scheduled to begin a five-date tour of small venues across the Highlands of Scotland that had been arranged two months earlier. Many roads were impassable. The first show (in Keith) had to be canceled, the remaining four suffered from poor attendance, and promoter Albert Bonici lost money.

It was an inauspicious start for the Beatles, who were hoping that the recent chart entry of their first single, "Love Me Do," and the imminent release of the follow-up, "Please Please Me," might bring them a measure of recognition beyond the local followings they had built over the previous few years in Liverpool and Hamburg.

The group's optimism, manager Brian Epstein's determination and producer George Martin's enthusiastic appraisal of the group's commercial potential were not widely shared.

The control of popular music in Britain remained, as it had throughout the 1950s, in the hands of a small number of agents, promoters and record labels (Decca, EMI, Philips and Pye), all of whom maintained a strong preference for London-based performers, an acceptance that musical trends in the U.K. were inevitably dictated by U.S. styles, a preference for the solo singer

Screaming Beatles fans in Manchester, England force a young police cadet to plug his ears.

PRESS ASSOCIATION VIA AP IMAGES

AP PHOTO

(or lead singer and backing group), a reluctance to depart from a musical policy characterized by familiarity and predictability, and an unquestioned assumption that the performer and the songwriter should be two separate people. The cozy lack of ambition that these beliefs created was seen in the persistent popularity of British pop stars such as Cliff Richard, Adam Faith, The Shadows, Craig Douglas, Billy Fury and Helen Shapiro, who happily met all the criteria demanded of them. (The Beatles toured with Shapiro, a prim teenager with a beehive hairdo, in February and March of 1963 as one of her opening acts.)

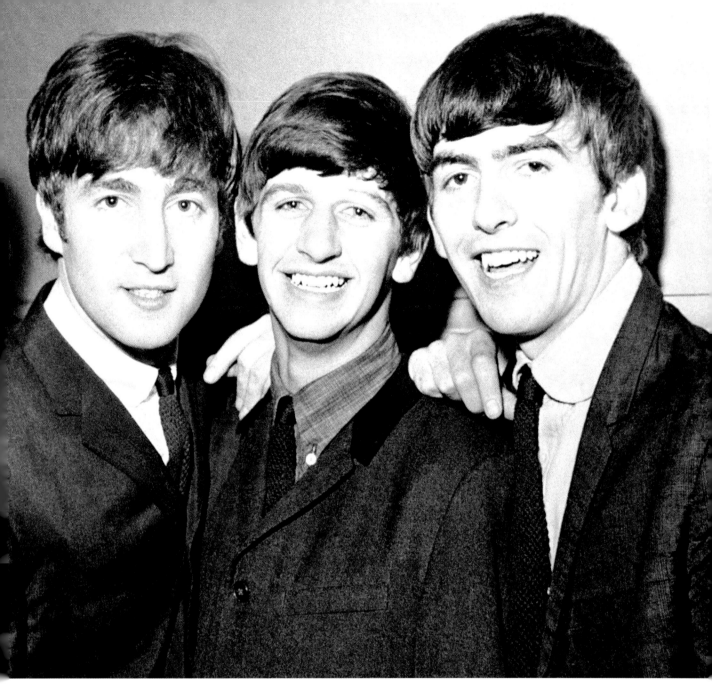

The notion that a group of four youngsters from deprived and distant Liverpool, that possessed no identifiable lead singer, that wrote and recorded its own songs, and that were managed by a local businessman with no experience in the entertainment industry might enjoy any meaningful success seemed absurd. The Beatles had been rejected out-of-hand by record companies Philips and Pye. Decca's blunt refusal to sign the group after its studio audition in January 1962, with the advice that guitar groups were "on the way out," typified the condescending and complacent attitudes faced by the band. Everywhere he turned, Epstein faced the same message: "The boys won't go, Mr. Epstein. We know these things. You have a good business in Liverpool. Stick to that."

Although the group had built up pockets of popularity, each success had come through slow and steady effort. The group's history dated back to 1956, when 16-year-old John Lennon, inspired by the sounds of Elvis Presley and Lonnie Donegan, persuaded a group of schoolfriends to join him in the formation of The Quarrymen skiffle group. By 1963, of the original line-up, only Lennon remained. As other members drifted away, pursued alternative ambitions or were fired, the arrivals of McCartney (1957), Harrison (1958) and Starr (1962) completed the group, which took the Beatles name in 1960.

At the start of 1963, it looked like John, Paul, George and Ringo would spend another year developing their craft and hoping for a big break.

Paul McCartney joined up with John Lennon in 1957, followed by George Harrison a year later and Ringo Starr in 1962.

The Beatles re-hearse for their appearance on the 1963 Royal Variety Performance in London.

Beatlemania in the U.K.

By the end of 1963, the Beatles were a phenom-enon. They had accumulated four No. 1 singles ("Please Please Me," "From Me To You," "She Loves You" and "I Want To Hold Your Hand") and two No. 1 albums (*Please Please Me* and *With the Beatles*). They had completed four nation-wide tours. They had hosted their own 15-part weekly BBC radio series (*Pop Goes the Beatles*), topped the bill on ITV's flagship entertainment program *Sunday Night at the London Palladium* and appeared before the royal family in the an-nual Royal Variety Performance. They had sanc-tioned the creation of a nationwide fan club, ap-proved the publication of an associated monthly magazine, *The Beatles Book*, whose circulation quickly reached 300,000, and established their own music publishing company. They had writ-ten chart hits for the Rolling Stones, Cilla Black, The Fourmost and Billy J. Kramer. To top it off, they had negotiated a three-picture film contract with United Artists. It was, by any standards, an astonishing and dramatic story.

Across the U.K., the unprecedented scenes of fan hysteria that surrounded the Beatles — dubbed Beatlemania by the press — quickly became the year's major news story, surpassing coverage of the Profumo scandal, in which a gov-ernment minister was forced to resign after lying to Parliament about his relationship with a pros-titute, and the Great Train Robbery, in which the equivalent of $73 million was stolen from the overnight mail train from Glasgow to London.

Authorship of the term Beatlemania was vari-ously claimed by the *Daily Mail*, the *Daily Mir-ror* and *Melody Maker*, all of whom pinpointed its first usage to October 1963, after the group's televised appearance on *Sunday Night at the Lon-don Palladium*.

But the phenomenon itself began to take shape long before that. On the Beatles' second U.K. tour of the year, when they were ostensibly supporting American pop stars Tommy Roe and Chris Mon-tez, the volume of screams during their perfor-mance and the swarm of fans at the end of every show were becoming increasingly apparent.

During their third tour, in May, the Beatles were elevated from supporting American croon-er Roy Orbison to sharing top billing with him and closing the show. Scenes of besieged theaters, overwhelmed police lines and fleets of waiting ambulances were supplemented by puzzling ac-counts of fan behavior. Jelly Babies bombarded the stage because George was said to like them

A Recipe for Mania

What could account for the Beatles' impact in a country where previous British performers had, at best, short-lived success? A managerial strategy that combined confidence and caution, a substantial promotional budget, the presence of two (later three) outstanding songwriters, and, of course, the music itself — simple, joyous, unadorned and uncomplicated, containing influences drawn from rock 'n' roll, pop, country and rhythm and blues traditions — were all factors that set up the Beatles for a magical run, but other elements added to the explosion that was Beatlemania.

The Beatles' visual imagery — the hair and the clothes — distanced the Fab Four from many of their competitors and allowed them to have a distinctive, unique identity. That identity was projected with great relish at the group's press conferences, where their spontaneous humor and self-deprecation stood in sharp contrast to other celebrities.

American fans, like their British counterparts, quickly formed ideas about the personalities of the four Beatles. They were incomplete and simplistic, but the conventional estimations of John (the cynical leader), Paul (the romantic charmer), George (the boy next door) and Ringo (the lovable clown) made the members of the band seem instantly familiar. The four distinct personalities allowed fans to enjoy multiple points of contact with the group in a way that had not been seen before in popular music.

An equally important part of Beatlemania was the United States itself. Specifically, three separate circumstances primed the U.S. for Beatlemania. First, the country's perception of itself had been fractured by the shock of John Kennedy's assassination in November 1963. The U.S. was desperately searching for ways in which a collective sense of identity might be restored. Second, 17-year-olds had become the largest single age group in the country, and they possessed a spending power not previously enjoyed by earlier generations. Third, rock 'n' roll had been largely replaced by inoffensive, middle-of-the-road music. (One of the acts that topped the singles charts in the months leading up to Beatlemania was the Singing Nun, who performed her hit "Dominique" in French. When "I Want to Hold Your Hand" reached No. 1, it deposed crooner Bobby Vinton's "There! I Said It Again," a song written in 1945.)

(in the U.S., these would be replaced with much harder jelly beans). Most bizarre were the reports of pools of urine soaking into the floor of the auditorium; crazed fans, it seemed, could not control their bladders.

However, the definitive moment in the birth of Beatlemania followed the release of "She Loves You" in August. Not only was it the first of the group's singles to sell more than 1 million copies in the U.K., but its "yeah, yeah, yeah" chorus and distinctive falsetto screams immediately became iconic shorthand indicators of the group and its music. As TV and radio appearances multiplied in the wake of the record's success, it was forcefully apparent that popular music had been dramatically disrupted.

The well-publicized scenes outside the London Palladium several weeks later were merely the capital's formal introduction to something that the rest of the country had known about for months. John Lennon's perennial encouragement to his fellow Beatles that they were destined for "the toppermost of the poppermost" had been emphatically vindicated.

The only topic of conversation in Britain at the end of 1963 was the Beatles.

The Beatles were everywhere in the U.K. in 1963, even guest starring on *Morecambe and Wise* (below), a popular variety show, in December.

AP PHOTO

EXPRESS NEWSPAPERS VIA AP IMAGES

Taking America

In the United States, the Beatles were more of a rumor than a band. Three Beatles' singles ("Please Please Me," "From Me To You" and "She Loves You") had been released on minor labels without success. The group's first U.K. album, *Please Please Me*, had been released as *Introducing the Beatles* and had suffered the same fate.

Despite these setbacks, a gradual awareness of the young band was beginning to develop: In May, Roy Orbison told Britain's *New Musical Express* that "the Beatles could be tops in America … but it will need careful handling." In June, Del Shannon's version of "From Me To You," the first American cover of a Beatles song, reached No. 77 on the Billboard singles chart.

In November, *Time* carried a story presenting British Beatlemania as "the new madness caused by a wild rhythm-and-blues quartet called the Beatles." In December, the *New York Times* reported the sensational, if misleading, news that "they are fighting all over Britain. Often there is a pitched battle, with broken legs, cracked ribs and bloody noses … the cause of this shattering of the English peace is a phenomenon called the Beatles." Also in December, *CBS Evening News* contained a brief item about Beatlemania in Britain.

In America

George Harrison was the only Beatle to have visited the U.S. before the Beatles flew to New York. In September 1963, he had paid a brief visit to his sister, Louise, who lived in St. Louis with her American husband. Two years earlier, Ringo Starr had visited the U.S. Consulate in Liverpool to discuss a possible emigration to Houston but had been deterred by the length and complexity of the formal application process.

Tchotchke-mania

Among the Beatles merchandise and memorabilia marketed in 1964 were inflatable dolls, canned breath, masks, wigs, pillows, nighties, bubble bath, table lamps, perfume, egg cups and wallpaper. Among the products rejected were sanitary towels and knives.

AP PHOTO

ley's "Hound Dog" / "Don't Be Cruel" — had ever managed the same feat.

The sense of rolling momentum gathered pace: Buoyed by the promise of three consecutive appearances on the *Ed Sullivan Show* and two concerts at New York's prestigious Carnegie Hall, invigorated by the news that "I Want To Hold Your Hand" (released Dec. 26, 1963) had climbed to the top of the U.S. singles charts, and assisted by a relentless publicity campaign on New York's WABC, WINS and WMCA radio stations, the Beatles flew into New York's Kennedy International Airport on Feb. 7, 1964. (The airport had been renamed after the slain president just a month and a half earlier.)

Apart from their time in Hamburg, the group's only previous foreign visits had been to Sweden and France, where reaction to the Beatles was generally positive but restrained. From the outset, America was different: Ringo Starr wryly observed that their reception was "just like Britain — only ten times bigger." He later expanded: "You all seem crazy here."

Previous demonstrations of adulation, such as those directed at Frank Sinatra in the 1940s and Presley in the 1950s, were dwarfed by a phenomenon that was built upon the premise and promise of fun. And the evident fact that the Beatles themselves shared in the fun increased its potency. The appeal of Sinatra and Presley reflected, in part, the glamorous and exclusive lives they led and the celebrity status they jealously guarded. In contrast, the Beatles were presented as familiar and likable youngsters who came from unremarkable backgrounds, who enjoyed

From Epstein's perspective, a hit single remained the essential ingredient in conquering America. In November, under pressure from its parent company EMI, Capitol Records decided to distribute "I Want To Hold Your Hand" and to back its release with an unprecedented $50,000 promotional program. The label's executives approved the budget after learning that the single was the first in U.K. history to have advance sales of more than 1 million copies. Even in the vastly larger U.S. market, only one record — Elvis Pres-

The Beatles and the United States

Jan. 11: "Please Please Me" / "Ask Me Why" is released in the U.K. It gathers momentum and tops the British charts in February.

Feb. 7: "Please Please Me" / "Ask Me Why" is released in the U.S. by Vee-Jay. It has some local success in Chicago but is otherwise a commercial failure.

Feb. 12: The Beatles go on tour supporting Helen Shapiro. They are one of many bands that play before the headliner, and they typically play four songs each night.

1963

LIBRARY OF CONGRESS

Jan. 11: George Wallace is inaugurated as governor of Alabama. He pledges, "Segregation today, segregation tomorrow and segregation forever."

Feb. 11: At a marathon recording session, the Beatles record many of the songs on the *Please Please Me* album, including "I Saw Her Standing There" and John's raucous, sore-throated version of "Twist and Shout," recorded at the end of the session.

Feb. 28: While on the Shapiro tour, Lennon and McCartney pen "From Me to You" in the back of the tour bus.

what they were doing, and who shared the same interests and ambitions as their audiences.

Given the irresistible force with which the Beatles had dismantled and rebuilt perceptions of popular music in Britain, it seems — from a distance of 50 years — surprising that there were some who failed to recognize the immediate significance of their arrival in America or the lasting implications of their music. *Newsweek* declared that "musically, they are a near-disaster … their lyrics are a catastrophe." However, such dissenting voices were rare. Bob Dylan had no hesitation in nominating the Beatles as the biggest single influence in his own transition from folk to rock: "I knew they were pointing the direction where music had to go." For their part, the Beatles were captivated by the brash consumerism and the unflagging pace of daily activities in America.

A Band Apart

The Beatles' career was, of course, grounded in their music. But in many ways, the personality and look of the Beatles was as important — and, in 1964, as memorable — as their sound. At Epstein's first meeting with them at Liverpool's Cavern Club, he noted their "very considerable magnetism and indefinable charm," and although Martin was intrigued by the group's audition tapes, it was not until he met the Beatles in Abbey Road Studios that he decided to offer them a recording contract: "They did not come alive until you saw them."

In an era when long hair on men was widely seen as a sign of delinquency or homosexuality, the Beatles' casual, fringed hairstyles and collarless jackets attracted as much attention as their songs. In Britain and America, their idiosyncra-

The Fab Four read fan mail in a Paris hotel room in 1964.

March 9: The Beatles kick off a tour in support of Americans Tommy Roe and Chris Montez. The Beatles quickly upstage the unhappy Americans, who are booed and jeered by Beatles' fans.

April 8: Julian Lennon is born in Liverpool. Several days later John goes to the hospital to meet his son.

May 18: The Beatles start their tour with Roy Orbison. Originally scheduled to be the headliner, Orbison gracefully allows the Beatles to take the top slot.

April 8: *Lawrence of Arabia* is named Best Picture at the Academy Awards.

May 8: *Dr. No,* the first James Bond film, is released in the U.S.

May 27: *The Freewheelin' Bob Dylan* is released and catapults the young folksinger to stardom. "Blowin' in the Wind" is covered by Peter, Paul and Mary and becomes a youth anthem.

sies of appearance and demeanor were, as Epstein had foreseen, a key element in making the Beatles as recognizable to those with no interest in their music as they were to their most devoted fans. Some commentators suspected that such "gimmickry" would limit the Beatles' ability to enjoy anything more than a temporary popularity. In the *Saturday Evening Post*, Vance Packard wrote, "The Beatles are so dependent upon their visual appeal that there is a question whether they can sustain the craze … crazes tend to die a horribly abrupt death."

The Beatles' first visit was limited to two weeks on the East Coast, a blitz of photo opportunities, personal appearances, media interviews and live performances. Fewer than 15,000 fans saw the band perform. Nevertheless, by the time the Beatles returned to the U.K., America had succumbed, and with even greater speed than Britain the previous year. The re-released "She Loves You" was at No. 2 in the singles chart behind "I Want To Hold Your Hand." The following week, these songs were joined in the top 10 by "Please Please Me." In early April, Beatles songs occupied the top five positions in the top 100, plus another seven positions lower on the chart.

To the Toppermost and Beyond

Recording commitments, the filming of their first movie and concert dates in Europe, Hong Kong, Australia and New Zealand prevented the Beatles from returning to the U.S. until mid-August 1964, when they embarked on their first nationwide tour. Despite the group's six-month absence, Beatlemania had only expanded.

The unparalleled sales of their singles and albums, the release in more than 500 theaters of *A Hard Day's Night*, the countless serializations of their life stories in newspapers and magazines and the flood of associated merchandise had primed audience anticipation to an almost unbearable level. The explosion of excitement ignited by their return ensured that the 27 concerts in five weeks across the U.S. and Canada was not simply a musical tour but a triumphant victory parade.

The Beatles toured the U.S. again in 1965, and then again in 1966. At the end of their third North American tour, mired in controversy over Lennon's comment that the Beatles were more popular than Jesus Christ, they resolved to abandon live performance and focus their creative energies on recording in the studio. Doubts about the wisdom of their decision disappeared the following year when they released *Sgt. Pepper's Lonely Hearts Club Band*. When Epstein died in 1967, they established Apple, their own management company, in an attempt to fill the void his absence had created. They dabbled in film, Apple foundered, they argued, they continued to record, they sought enlightenment with the Maharishi Mahesh Yogi, they argued again, they spoke openly about their use of drugs. The familiar Fab Four vanished in a psychedelic swirl of beards, mustaches, glasses, beads and kaftans. Ringo acted. John met Yoko. Paul met Linda. George forged new musical friendships with Ravi Shankar, Eric Clapton and Bob Dylan.

In 1969, during rehearsals for *Let It Be*, the Beatles gave a final impromptu concert on the rooftop of the Apple offices in London and, still arguing, they decided to call it a day. They took American

The Beatles and the United States

June 16: Cosmonaut Valentina Tereshkova becomes the first woman in space, a reminder of the U.S.S.R.'s lead in the Space Race.

Aug. 23: "She Loves You" / "I'll Get You" is released in the U.K. It sells 1 million copies by November.

Sept. 15: A new season of TV kicks off. Returning favorites include *My Favorite Martian*, *The Andy Griffith Show* and *The Beverly Hillbillies*.

1963

June 12: Civil rights activist Medgar Evers is assassinated in Jackson, Miss., capturing national attention. Evers is buried in Arlington National Cemetery a week later.

June 26: President Kennedy delivers his "Ich bin ein Berliner" speech in West Berlin.

LIBRARY OF CONGRESS

Aug. 28: Martin Luther King Jr. delivers his "I Have a Dream" speech from the steps of the Lincoln Memorial during the March on Washington.

Sept. 15: The 16th Street Baptist Church is bombed in Birmingham, Ala. Four girls are killed.

wives, bought American homes, worked with American producers and musicians and embarked on solo careers, coming together only occasionally. In 1980, Lennon was murdered in New York. In 2001, Harrison died in Los Angeles.

Fifty years after Pan Am Flight 101 brought the Beatles to America, the reverberations from their arrival are still sounding. Forever associated with the century's most beguiling decade, the Beatles transcended popular music to become historical in their own right. Like Picasso in modern art or Shakespeare in classical theater, their importance and influence in popular music is unique. In 1970, in the bitter aftermath of the Beatles' disintegration, John Lennon claimed that "the dream is over." For once he was wrong. **O**

Ian Inglis is a Visiting Fellow at Northumbria University, Newcastle upon Tyne, U.K. His three books on the Beatles include The Beatles in Hamburg. *His favorite Beatles' song is "Girl," an overlooked masterpiece.*

On Feb. 9, 1964, Americans watched the Beatles perform five songs live on the *Ed Sullivan Show*, sparking Beatlemania in the United States.

Sept. 16: "She Loves You" / "I'll Get You" is released in the U.S. by Swan Records. The record flops.

Oct. 31: The Beatles return from Sweden and are greeted by delirious fans at London's Heathrow Airport. Ed Sullivan happens to be at the airport to witness the scene and immediately decides to book the band on his show.

Nov. 29: "I Want to Hold Your Hand" / "This Boy" is released in the U.K. It has over 1 million advance orders.

Dec. 26: "I Want to Hold Your Hand" / "This Boy" is released in the U.S. Backed by a huge promotional budget, it will be the Beatles' first U.S. hit.

Oct. 13: The Beatles appear on the U.K. television show *London Night at the Palladium* in an event that cements their status as a cultural phenomenon.

Nov. 22: President Kennedy is shot and killed during a presidential motorcade in Dallas. Doctors announce him dead at 1:00 p.m. Lee Harvey Oswald is arrested later in the afternoon.

Nov. 25: An estimated 800,000 Americans line the streets of Washington, D.C. for Kennedy's funeral procession. Millions more in the U.S. and around the world watch on television.

The Beal

On Feb. 9, 1964, music in America changed forever when the Beatles appeared on the *Ed Sullivan Show*.

BY GLENN GASS

The Beatles on the *Ed Sullivan Show* ... 50 years ago. That milestone is hard to grasp for those of us who remember it — not exactly like yesterday, but certainly not like a half-century ago.

The Beatles performing on the *Ed Sullivan Show.*

More than 73 million television viewers watched the Beatles' first appearance on the *Ed Sullivan Show* in 1964, the largest TV audience ever recorded by Nielson.

For those too young to remember, it's probably hard to even imagine a time when an entire generation watched the same live television show and was changed by the same thing at the same time. No repeat broadcasts later in the week, no DVR, no Facebook, no YouTube … one big moment, and you didn't dare miss it.

You would likely have seen the Beatles on the *Ed Sullivan Show* even if you didn't know it was coming (though we all did).

Sunday Nights with Ed Sullivan

The *Ed Sullivan Show* was a Sunday night family ritual long before the Beatles came along, a vaudeville-style variety show featuring comedy acts, classical pianists, trapeze artists, exotic dancers, singers, movie stars, magicians, musical theater troupes (including, immediately following the Beatles, future Monkee Davy Jones and the cast of "Oliver" and Topo Gigio, the talking mouse — you had to be there).

Sullivan introduced each act with a flat dead-pan delivery more in keeping with a high-school talent show than a major television network. In his attempt to have something for everyone, the range of acts he booked was ludicrously varied. Luckily for us, he included acts for "the youngsters," as Sullivan put it, and the Beatles could not have hoped for a bigger boost to their American ambitions. The *Ed Sullivan Show* was the most important show on television for an aspiring act

Sullivan and the Beatles

The Beatles appeared on the *Ed Sullivan Show* four times. They appeared on three consecutive Sundays in February 1964 and again in August 1965:

● On Feb. 9, the band performed "All My Loving," "Till There Was You," "She Loves You," "I Saw Her Standing There" and "I Want to Hold Your Hand."

● On Feb. 16, the show was broadcast from Miami Beach. The Beatles opened with "She Loves You," "This Boy" and "All My Loving." The show closed with "I Saw Her Standing There," "From Me to You" and "I Want to Hold Your Hand."

● The Beatles' Feb. 23 appearance was on tape (from two weeks earlier before the live television show). They performed three songs: "Twist and Shout," "Please Please Me" and "I Want to Hold Your Hand."

● On Aug. 14, 1965, the Beatles performed "I Feel Fine," "I'm Down," "Act Naturally," "Ticket to Ride," "Yesterday" and "Help!"

In subsequent years, the Beatles gave Sullivan exclusive clips of the band performing songs, including "Paperback Writer," "Rain," "Penny Lane" and "Strawberry Fields Forever."

of any kind. The exposure it offered could ignite a career and, as with the Beatles, turn a performance into a cultural event, thanks to the sheer enormity of the audience.

Sullivan was always on the prowl for talent, and we were always watching to see what gems he might come up with between the dancing elephants and Anacin commercials.

In late 1963 when Sullivan signed the group, still completely unknown in America, to an unprecedented three-week run the following February, he forced Capitol Records to end a year of foot-dragging in America and get behind the Beatles' next single, "I Want To Hold Your Hand." The record went to No. 1 in January 1964, just in time to whip up excitement for the Sullivan appearance.

Nothing Else Mattered

And what excitement. That name! That hair! Those accents! Strange as it now seems, the music was not really much of an issue, beyond the climactic head-and-hair-shaking "woos" (cue screaming girls) and Paul's octave leap on the word "hand," which jumped out like a jack-in-the-box no longer able to contain its excite-ment. No one considered the music to have any real depth or, Lord knows, lasting value.

All around the country kids sat awkwardly by their parents that Sunday night watching their world change while the adults rolled their eyes and made derisive comments. ("How long do you think *they* will last?") Yes, there was a time when parents hated the Beatles, or were bemused at best, as if the Beatles were just a long-haired sideshow routine.

Our parents' cluelessness only made the Beatles more special, more wholly ours. The next day at school all anyone had to say was "Well?" and the conversation immediately turned to the Beatles: What did you think? Which one was which? Was that hair real? Which one was the leader? Could you understand a word they said? Liverpool?

Nothing but the Beatles seemed to matter or even exist. It was a new world, and we knew it — not in retrospect, but right then. The world had shifted on its axis, and our time had begun. A New York fan held up a sign reading, "Elvis is dead! Long Live the Beatles!" And it was true: The '50s and rock's first era were over. The king was dead. Long live the new kings, the Beatles.

The Beatles' appearance on the *Ed Sullivan*

All four Beatles' appearances on the *Ed Sullivan Show* were in black and white. The show switched to color the week after the band's last appearance.

AP PHOTO

Photographers surround the Fab Four as they rehearse at CBS' Studio 50.

Show on Feb. 9, 1964 was one of the great television moments of all time, a one-two punch of aural and visual exhilaration that catapulted the Beatles directly into orbit. It also marked the true arrival of the '60s, as the baby boomers rumbled to life and began the transformation into the Woodstock Nation. That journey was driven in no small part by our emulation of the Beatles, beginning with hairstyles and ending with a nonconformist worldview in complete opposition to the values of our parents, our government and most other symbols of authority.

The Beatles, on that Sunday night, were the first thing that truly united us — the first thing that gave "us" meaning — and they remained a constant through the ever-changing '60s, the beating heart of the counter-culture. They were like everyone's incredibly cool older brothers, telling us not to worry about mom and dad and bringing us to each new experience, each new reality, with the reassuring message that there was room enough for all. It was thrilling, joyful and oddly comforting: You knew the Beatles would never let you down or lead you astray, and they never did.

The timing of the Beatles' invasion of America couldn't have been better, between the enduring doldrums of the Kennedy assassination and a musical culture stuck in reverse. It seemed like only an invasion of aliens from outer space could possibly make things exciting again.

AP PHOTO / MUSEUM OF TELEVISION & RADIO

Star Maker

The *Ed Sullivan Show* was a variety show that aired on CBS from 1948 to 1971. Although the show featured acts of all kinds, it is credited with airing breakthrough performances by musical legends before they were stars. Most notable are Elvis Presley (photo at left is of his Sept. 9, 1956 appearance), the Beatles, the Supremes, the Rolling Stones, the Beach Boys, the Jackson 5, Janis Joplin and The Doors.

A New Kind of Rock 'n' Roll

And they came! The Beatles, with that impossibly long hair (Were they wigs? Could male hair actually grow that long?) and those indecipherable accents, seemed like a new breed of young people full of life and energy. The music they made sounded sleek, new and immediately right. It was rock 'n' roll but in a brand-new guise.

And they were a group without a leader, a group of equals. It seemed strange indeed, as we struggled to figure out which one to watch, before we realized they were four parts of a whole (the "four-headed monster," as Mick Jagger put it).

The lead guitar player was elevated to a starring role, standing in the middle, but he didn't have a microphone, forcing him to roam over to join one of the other singers to add his harmonies. It was a true joy to watch George on "All My Loving," the first song they played on the show, as he joined John for harmony "oohs" then played a wonderfully concise guitar solo before joining Paul to sing lead harmonies on the verse — the ultimate swingman on the ultimate team.

Meanwhile, the two main singers were on opposite sides, beautifully symmetrical thanks to Paul's left-handed bass playing. And the drummer — Ringo! At least we knew which one he was, thanks to his name and nose. Yes, he was in the back, as usual for drummers, but on a riser and always visible.

They looked stunning, perfect, like a whole world compressed into all that mattered. "I Want To Hold Your Hand" was already a No. 1

hit, but seeing the Beatles fired our collective imaginations in a way that a mere record never could (until *Sgt. Pepper's Lonely Hearts Club Band*, anyway, three insanely long years later).

They seemed to love singing together and seemed to love each other in a joyous, natural way without a trace of show business phoniness. They were the very image of youth and fun, and we all desperately wanted to be a part of it. We ditched our acoustic folk guitars and formed bands if we could. If not, we just yanked on our hair to get it to grow faster and strummed badminton racquets as we sang along to those amazing records.

Sullivan's set added to the image of a perfect, seamless whole, surrounding the Beatles with a circle of huge arrows pointing inward as if ready to set off a nuclear implosion. Something even bigger detonated that February night. We couldn't have imagined the Beatles in our wildest dreams, and then we took one look and shouted a collective, "Yeah, yeah, yeah!". **O**

Glenn Gass is a professor at Indiana University, where he teaches courses that he developed on the history of rock music, including a course on the Beatles that he has offered since 1982, the longest-running course on the Beatles in existence. His favorite Beatles song is whichever one he's listening to at the moment, although if he had to pick, it would be "In My Life."

Speed skater Terry McDermott, a barber by trade, pretends to lop off Paul's locks as his bandmates and Sullivan look on in mock horror.

Twist and Shout

AP PHOTO

The Beatles' U.S. tours went from triumphant to frustrating — and then were done.

BY GILLIAN G. GAAR

Sixty-six shows. That's how many opportunities fans had to see the Beatles live in North America. Those 66 shows (which included nine shows in Canada) were played in just 33 cities over the course of three summers — 1964 to 1966. Anyone who can lay claim to having seen a Beatles show in North America is very lucky indeed.

EXPRESS NEWSPAPERS VIA AP IMAGES

The Beatles took America by storm with multi-city tours in the summers of 1964, 1965 and 1966. At far left, the band arrives at Kennedy International Airport in New York to play at Shea Stadium.

In 1964, the Beatles performed in huge venues in front of massive crowds like the Memorial Coliseum in Dallas (above), the Las Vegas Convention Center (right) and the Coliseum in Washington, D.C. (opposite page).

By the time the Beatles reached these shores, their live show was tailored for maximum impact. The days of sweating through six-hour sets in the clubs of Hamburg were long gone. The shows during the Beatles' North American tours lasted barely 30 minutes — even less if they played faster. Their amps (a then-hefty 100 watts) were hopelessly inadequate to overcome the screams that erupted while the group was playing. And though the band's music progressed fantastically in the studio during those three years, that wasn't the case with their live shows. Claiming that their songs had become too complex to perform live, the Beatles didn't feature a single track from their most recent album, *Revolver*, during their 1966 tour.

Nights to Remember

For all their inadequacies, the shows were nonetheless monumental occasions in the lives of those fortunate enough to see them. "You were there, in the same room, hearing them in person, in all their greatness," recalls fan Judie Sims, who saw the group in both 1964 and 1966. "It was awesome!" And for the Beatles, the tours provid-

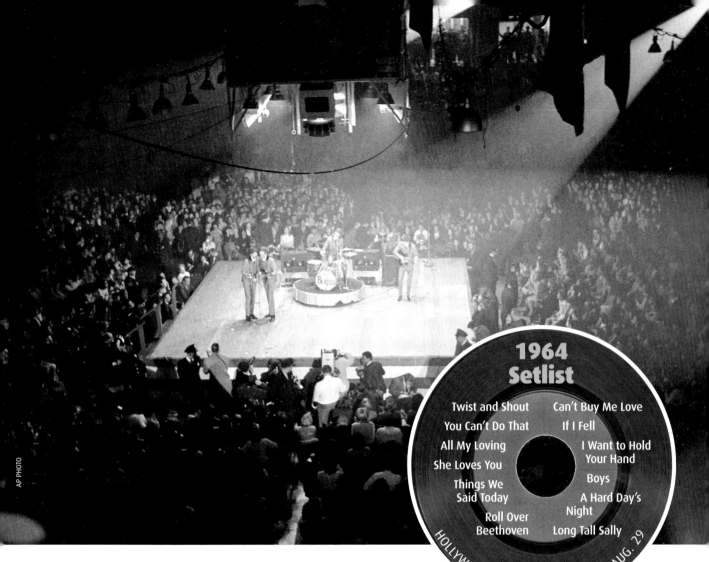

1964 Setlist

Twist and Shout

You Can't Do That

All My Loving

She Loves You

Things We Said Today

Roll Over Beethoven

Can't Buy Me Love

If I Fell

I Want to Hold Your Hand

Boys

A Hard Day's Night

Long Tall Sally

HOLLYWOOD BOWL, LOS ANGELES — AUG. 29

ed a welcome infusion of energy, at least initially. "When the Beatles played in America for the first time, they were already old hands," John Lennon recalled in 1980. "It was pure craftsmanship. Only the excitement of the American kids, the American scene, made it come alive."

Part of the excitement came from the huge crowds the band played to. In England and Europe, the Beatles played theaters and concert halls. On their North American tours, they played stadiums and ballparks, most with a capacity of 10,000-plus. They were the first band that showed a rock act could consistently draw a stadium-sized crowd. And their success opened the doors for the future stadium acts that followed: the Rolling Stones, The Who and Led Zeppelin. Beyond the Beatles' music, their tours helped change the music industry forever.

The trade-off was that it was impossible to maintain the kind of intimacy the Beatles had previously enjoyed with their audiences when they played clubs. Over time, the shows became less about the music and more about being there, less of a musical experience and more of a rit-ual ("bloody tribal rites," in Lennon's words). The fans came, screamed and waved in the frantic hope that their favorite Beatle would somehow see them from the stage. "George looked right at me," Sims says about her first Beatles concert in Philadelphia in 1964. "I will never forget that. My cousin and I cried after it was over."

1964: Beatlemania, American Style

The Beatles eventually tired of what George Harrison liked to call "the mania" surrounding the group's tours. But when they arrived for their first North American tour in August 1964, they were still enthusiastic, riding the giddy heights of the first flush of Beatlemania, American style. They had the No. 1 album in the country with *A Hard Day's Night*, while the album's title track had just left the top spot in the singles chart. Ahead of them lay their most extensive North American tour. From August 19 to September 20, they played a total of 32 shows.

Twist and Shout
She's a Woman
I Feel Fine
Dizzy Miss Lizzy
Ticket to Ride
Everybody's Trying to Be My Baby

Can't Buy Me Love
Baby's in Black
Act Naturally
A Hard Day's Night
Help
I'm Down

SHEA STADIUM, NEW YORK CITY — AUG. 15

More than 55,000 people saw the Beatles perform 12 songs at Shea Stadium in 1965.

The Beatles were the hottest showbiz act in the world, and everybody wanted a piece of the action. San Francisco hoped to throw a ticker-tape parade for the band to mark the tour's beginning, but Harrison was quick to demur, not wanting to make himself a target in a country whose president had been gunned down by a sniper's rifle less than a year earlier. It wasn't an unfounded fear; during the tour, bomb threats were made in Las Vegas and Dallas. Ringo received a death threat when the group played Montreal (a police officer was enlisted to sit by his side during the shows to protect him).

Footage of the tour shows that when the Beatles weren't on stage, they were constantly under siege, from fans trying to touch them ("I'd like to get a piece of the Beatles, at least!" an outraged male fan howled to one reporter), dignitaries vying for access to them, and reporters trying to squeeze in one more question ("Leonard Bernstein likes your music. How do you like him?" Paul: "Very good. He's, you know, great"). Being constantly pushed, as a character in *A Hard Day's Night* memorably put it, between "a train and a room, a car and a room, and a room and a room."

"It was just one long hustle," Starr recalled to biographer Hunter Davies. "You could see [people] thinking … what's the matter with you, you've only worked half an hour today. But we'd probably traveled 2,000 miles since the last half and not eaten or slept properly for two weeks."

And that half hour contained the same 12 songs night after night, the band buzzing through them at high speed, hyped up on adrenaline. Ironically, what was arguably the tour's most important moment would turn out to a non-musical one. On Aug. 28, after playing the first of two shows at Forest Hills Tennis Stadium in New York, the Beatles invited Bob Dylan to visit them at the Delmonico Hotel. When Dylan arrived, he produced marijuana and suggested they all light up.

Though it's been said Dylan thus "introduced" the Beatles to pot, Harrison later admitted they had actually smoked it before in Liverpool. But this time was different. It was the moment pot became their recreational drug of choice, an influence that would soon make itself felt in the band's music. The evening was also a rare opportunity for the Beatles to meet someone who was a genuine musical peer (they'd also met Fats Domino when they played New Orleans) and marked the beginning of their longstanding friendship with Dylan.

1965: The High Water Mark

The Beatles' 1965 North American tour was their shortest on the continent, just 15 shows in 20 days. And it began with one of the most memorable dates in their career: an Aug. 15 concert at Shea Stadium in Queens before a record audience of 55,600. The show's promoter, Sid Bernstein (who had booked the Beatles' Carnegie Hall concerts in February 1964), boasted that he didn't even have a written contract for the momentous gig.

"There were no lawyers involved," he said. "It was just Brian [Epstein] and I on the phone making the deal. You know what I would get for a contract, if I'd ever had a copy of it? Probably $100,000 at Sotheby's."

Twelve cameras were on hand to capture the show for the TV documentary *The Beatles at Shea Stadium*. It remains the best film record of the Beatles' live act, despite the fact that the band rerecorded most of the soundtrack later in the studio. The 55,000 fans in attendance formed the largest audience a rock band had ever drawn

up to that point. The Beatles' sense of wonder as they first took the stage was clear as they looked around wide-eyed while hundreds of flashbulbs popped futilely in the distance (the stage was set up at second base, with the audience kept safely in the stands). By the set's end, the Beatles were dripping with sweat, stomping through the closing number, "I'm Down," before leaping into the getaway car parked at the side of the stage and driving off into the night.

The 1965 Shea Stadium concert was undeniably the high water mark of their touring years. "Fantastic, the most exciting [show] we've done," as John later recalled, adding, "they could almost hear us as well."

A Fan's Eye View

Pat Mancuso was 15 years old when she first saw a film clip of the Beatles on *The Jack Paar Show* in December 1963, dismissing them as "funny looking." She changed her mind the following month while attending the last taping of *American Bandstand* in Philadelphia prior to the show moving to Los Angeles. Dick Clark spun "She Loves You" and "I Want to Hold Your Hand." Mancuso recalls that, "Something clicked inside me. I think it was the excitement. They were different."

Seven months later, Mancuso was in the audience when the Beatles played Atlantic City. "I sat in row 125 or something," she says. "The only time I saw them was if I jumped up and down on my chair at the right time. I remember thinking 'Who cares if I can see them? I'm breathing the same air.' I screamed so much that I didn't have a voice the next morning."

The following year, Mancuso became president of the Official George Harrison Fan Club. She and her friends proudly sported homemade "I Love George" buttons when they attended the Shea Stadium show.

"The Shea 1965 concert was amazing," she says. "I had never been in a baseball stadium before, so I was in awe over the size of it. The fans were fainting like flies and cops were carrying them away. One girl escaped the stands and ran toward the Beatles and then the cops ran after her; when they caught her, everybody booed. My father took pictures of me and my friends freaking out. I remember crying hysterically when the show was over."

Mancuso also attended the '66 Shea performance, sternly telling her friends they could only scream between the songs. "I don't think anybody listened — including me!" At the show in Philadelphia, she and her friend wore blue business suits with an embroidered Harrison fan club "GHFC" emblem on the sleeves; "It didn't really get us backstage, but I met [Beatles road manager] Mal Evans!"

AP PHOTO / EDDIE ADAMS

Mancuso later met Harrison in England and wrote the book *Do You Want to Know a Secret? The Story of the Official George Harrison Fan Club*. And she has vivid memories of what made the live experience different from watching archive footage: "The excitement. The sweat. The smell of popcorn. All the teenage drama — hysterical, fainting people! All you know is that 'Oh my God, the Beatles are right there!' And you want your favorite Beatle to look at you."

1966 Setlist

Rock & Roll Music
She's a Woman
If I Needed Someone
Day Tripper
Baby's in Black
I Feel Fine
Yesterday
I Wanna Be Your Man
Nowhere Man
Paperback Writer
Long Tall Sally

CANDLESTICK PARK, SAN FRANCISCO — AUG. 29

The summer of 1966 was the last time the Beatles toured in America. They wave to fans as they leave London for the U.S. (above). At right, they arrive at San Francisco to perform at Candlestick Park on Aug. 29, their final U.S. concert.

But their set lists were stuck in a rut; only three of the 12 songs they played each night were from 1965, and there was a surprisingly high number of cover songs in the set (three). The Beatles did not make any effort to perform anything that wasn't a rock 'n' roller. Their stage act was still for teenyboppers even though their music was leaving that era behind.

Two key events happened when the tour touched down in Los Angeles. While tripping on LSD around the pool on a rare day off, Lennon was sufficiently unnerved by actor Peter Fonda's stoned ramblings that "I know what it's like to be dead" that Lennon filed away the remark for use in a future song ("She Said, She Said"). And on the night of Aug. 27, they were ushered into the presence of the man who had so influenced them, Elvis Presley. The Beatles were so nervous they smoked pot beforehand, then loosened up enough to ask Presley, in a nice bit of foreshadowing, why

he had stopped giving concerts. (Presley replied that he was too tied up with his film career.)

At the time, the Beatles couldn't imagine being a viable act without performing live. "We couldn't stand not doing personal appearances; we'd get bored," Lennon said. Yet they found that touring also hampered their studio work. After the 1964 North American tour, the Beatles went straight into a U.K. tour. With little spare time left in which to craft an album of original material, they fell back on cover songs when they recorded their next album, *Beatles For Sale* (the songs were spread over the albums *Beatles '65* and *Beatles VI* in the U.S.). The shorter tours in 1965 allowed the band to more fully engage in writing and recording new music, and *Rubber Soul* was the happy result, followed by "Paperback Writer" and the masterful album *Revolver*.

1966: The Grind

By 1966 there was little incentive to do an extensive tour; between Aug. 12 and 29, the Beatles performed 19 shows. And they arrived embroiled in controversy, due to Lennon's remarks to a British journalist about Christianity earlier in the year ("It will vanish and shrink … We're more popular than Jesus now"). He apologized at the tour's first press conference, but questions about his comments dogged the rest of the tour, and death threats were made as well. When a firecracker exploded during the group's second show in Memphis, each Beatle instantly looked at the others, fearful that one of them had been shot.

The tensions cast a pall over the tour, and it was noted that ticket sales were also down. A return engagement at Shea Stadium failed to sell out; promoter Bernstein told *The New York Times* that it was a disappointment, "but I think I knew it was coming." Grinding through the same 12 songs that no one could hear had become tiresome. "We got worse as musicians, playing the same old junk every day," Harrison told Hunter Davies. "There was no satisfaction at all." Bootleg recordings of the Beatles' shows that year confirm that their playing was lackluster.

Even McCartney, the Beatle most devoted to touring, said, "Now even America was beginning to pall because of the conditions of touring and because we'd done it so many times." So the band decided that their last ever show would be at the tour's end, Aug. 29 at Candlestick Park in San Francisco. After McCartney wailed through "Long Tall Sally," the band put down their instruments. The Beatles' touring days were over. Harrison later recalled thinking, "This is going to be such a relief — not to have to go through that madness anymore."

Just Another Memory

The Beatles' touring years live on in official releases like *The Beatles Anthology* DVDs. Still, for an act of the Beatles' stature, it's odd that they have yet to release an album or DVD of a complete show (several performances circulate as bootleg recordings). But the Beatles never looked back on their touring days with much fondness; when they spoke of their best years as live performers, they always looked back to their pre-fame period. "We always missed the club dates 'cause that's when we were playing music," Lennon told *Rolling Stone*, "but as soon as we made it, the edges were knocked off … the Beatles' music died then, as musicians."

Still, those who saw the band can't forget the sheer joy they experienced. And touring was a large part of what took the Beatles from regional fame in Britain to international stardom. Their explosive success also singlehandedly saved rock music, which had been on the wane in the U.S. in favor of surf music or dance fads like The Twist.

The Lost Live Album

If Capitol Records had had their way, the Beatles' Aug. 23, 1964 show at Hollywood Bowl would have been their first live album. A mobile three-track unit recorded the entire 12-song set. In a year which saw Capitol release five Beatles albums, a live album would have put a final touch on a year of unprecedented success.

Acetates of the show were made for the Beatles to listen to, but the group, and producer George Martin, felt the sound was abysmal compared to what they could achieve in the studio. A brief excerpt of "Twist and Shout" ended up being included on the 1964 documentary album *The Beatles' Story*, which mainly consisted of interviews and clips from press conferences.

Capitol tried again the following year, recording the two shows the Beatles played at the Hollywood Bowl on Aug. 29 and 30, 1965. But the band was no more amenable to the idea of releasing a live album than it had been before, though the Aug. 30 performance of "Twist and Shout" was used in *The Beatles at Shea Stadium* television special. Capitol also pushed the idea of a live album in both 1966 and in 1971, but still met with refusals.

When the Beatles' contract with the label expired in 1976, Capitol was free to release the band's music however it wanted and plans for a live album finally went ahead. George Martin was brought in to produce, and a composite performance of 13 songs, drawn from all three shows, was released in May 1977 as *The Beatles at the Hollywood Bowl*. The album reached the No. 2 spot on the charts in the U.S. and remains the only official live album released by the group — though it has yet to appear on CD. ◘

After the Beatles, rock was never again regarded as a flash-in-the-pan novelty. During their turn on the world's stages, they transformed rock from a teen craze to big business. Beatles concerts weren't just shows, they were bona fide events. And as a song on a future album would put it, a splendid time was guaranteed for all. ◘

Gillian G. Gaar is the author of 100 Things Beatles Fans Should Know & Do Before They Die. *Her favorite Beatles' song? It's a tie between "She Loves You" and "Eleanor Rigby."*

the Beatles Facts

600 MILLION

Number of Beatles albums sold worldwide. In the United States, the band tops the list with 177 million albums sold, ahead of Elvis Presley with 134.5 million.

SIMPLY SIMPSONS

Three Beatles appeared on three separate episodes of *The Simpsons*.
- **Ringo** appeared in a 1991 episode called "Brush with Greatness."
- **George** appeared in a 1993 episode called "Homer's Barbershop Quartet."
- **Paul** appeared in a 1995 episode called "Lisa The Vegetarian."

April 4, 1964

The week the Beatles occupied the first five positions on the Billboard Hot 100 — the only group in rock 'n' roll history to achieve this feat:
1. "Can't Buy Me Love"
2. "Twist and Shout"
3. "She Loves You"
4. "I Want to Hold Your Hand"
5. "Please Please Me"

That same week, the band also had another seven records in the Hot 100, bringing the total to 12 for the week.

20

The number of No. 1 singles the Beatles racked up in the U.S. — a Billboard record that still stands. In 2000, a compilation album was released, simply titled *1*, which featured every No. 1 single released in the U.S. and U.K.

19

How many No. 1 albums the Beatles had in the Billboard Top 200 charts — a record.

Films Starring the Beatles
- *A Hard Day's Night* (1964)
- *Help!* (1965)
- *Magical Mystery Tour* (1967)
- *Yellow Submarine* (1968)

Documentaries
- *The Beatles: The First U.S. Visit* (1991; re-edited version or 1964's *What's Happening! The Beatles in the U.S.A.*)
- *The Beatles at Shea Stadium* (1966)
- *Let It Be* (1970)

- *The Compleat Beatles* (1982)
- *The Beatles Anthology* (1996)
- *All Together Now* (2008)

AP PHOTO

and Figures

8

The number of consecutive No. 1 albums in the Billboard chart — another record for the Beatles.

 iTunes

In November 2010, the entire Beatles catalog became available on iTunes. In the first week, the band sold more than 2 million songs and 450,000 albums. The most downloaded songs that first week were:

"Here Comes the Sun"
"Come Together"
"Let it Be"
"In My Life"
"Blackbird"
"Something"

"With a Little Help From My Friends"
"Yesterday"
"Lucy in the Sky with Diamonds"
"Dear Prudence"

Rock Band

The Beatles: Rock Band music video game debuted in 2009. The game, developed by Harmonix Music Systems, published by MTV Games, and distributed by Electronic Arts, is the first band-centric game in the Rock Band series.

$25 MILLION

Earnings in 1964 alone from the Beatles' 15 records — 9 singles and 6 albums — that sold over 1 million copies each in the U.S. In 2013 dollars, the band's 1964 earnings would be almost $188 million.

Awards and Recognitions

● The film *Let It Be* (1970) won the 1971 Academy Award for Best Original Song Score.

● In the U.S., the Beatles have 7 Grammy Awards, 6 Diamond (more than 10 million in sales) albums, 24 Multi-Platinum (more than 2 million) albums, 39 Platinum (more than 1 million) albums and 45 Gold (more than 500,000) albums.

● In 1965, Queen Elizabeth II appointed Lennon, McCartney, Harrison and Starr Members of the Order of the British Empire (MBE).

● The Beatles were inducted into the Rock and Roll Hall of Fame in 1988.

THE BEATLES

What you'll find on the north side of the 7100 block of Marshfield Way on the Hollywood Walk of Fame.

THE Great Invasion

The Beatles kicked off a conquering wave of bands from Britain.

BY JAMES E. PERONE

The British Invasion started with a German assault. Britain suffered enormous devastation as a result of the German bombing campaigns during World War II. The relentless German Luftwaffe bombarded the major cities of Britain, destroying more than 1 million homes in London alone and killing upwards of 40,000 people.

George Harrison   Ringo Starr   Paul McCartney   John Lennon

Hair stylists fix the boys' hair on the set of *A Hard Day's Night*. George's stylist, Pattie Boyd, later becomes his wife.

Reporter Ed Rudy interviewed the band before their 1964 concert at Carnegie Hall. John Lennon said about their popularity, "We don't think we're gonna last forever. We just gonna have a good time while we last."

As George Harrison put it, "You couldn't get a cup of sugar, never mind a rock 'n' roll record."

The economic struggles heightened the country's long-standing social and economic class distinctions. It was in this environment that many of the musicians who played active roles in the British Invasion of 1964 grew up.

Skiffle Influence

It's no surprise that young Brits, needing an escape from the recovery around them, turned to American music. But the kind of music that eventually ignited the British Invasion was an unlikely one: skiffle, an early 20th-century, rural, African-American music associated with the banjo, acoustic guitar and inexpensive homemade instruments, such as the washboard (for rhythm) and single-string washtub or tea-chest bass. Acoustic blues, and eventually electric blues, supplanted skiffle before it had a chance to penetrate the larger musical culture in the United States.

In Britain, skiffle burst into widespread popularity in the early 1950s, primarily through the success of a Scottish singer-guitarist-banjoist

The German Luftwaffe nearly destroyed the Beatles' hometown of Liverpool during WWII.

Especially hard hit were industrial and shipping centers in the country's major cities. After London, the city that was the most often targeted by the Luftwaffe was an important port city where raw materials to support the war effort poured in through the docks. Its name: Liverpool.

The destruction of heavy industry and working-class neighborhoods and the massive loss of jobs created economic difficulties well into the 1950s.

After the war, skiffle became popular. Lonnie Donegan (above), the "King of Skiffle," inspired bands like the Rolling Stones (right) and The Who (opposite page).

named Lonnie Donegan, who was known for recordings such as "Rock Island Line," "John Henry" and "Wabash Cannonball." For working-class British youths who could not afford expensive musical instruments, skiffle clearly had an economic attraction. Not only that, but the American songs that skiffle bands performed often required only two or three chords.

Skiffle was easy to play; featured easy-to-remember, singable tunes; used inexpensive, homemade instruments; and emphasized bright tempos and rhythm — what more could you ask for? Not much, according to The Who's lead singer, Roger Daltrey, who suggested that Lonnie Donegan and the skiffle style was the one thing that convinced him as a youth that he, too, could become a musician.

According to veteran British musician Ron Ryan, formerly a member of The Walkers and a songwriter for The Dave Clark Five, "every street in London had a skiffle band" between about 1955 and 1957. Ultimately, nearly every member of nearly every band that made an impact as part of the British Invasion performed in a skiffle band at some point in the late 1950s, including Roger Daltrey, Pete Townshend, Jimmy Page, Van Morrison, Mick Jagger and all four members of the Beatles.

The tunes that skiffle bands performed were largely drawn from American folk, country and rural African-American traditions. As a result, skiffle introduced Britain to musical forms and cultures that fundamentally differed from those favored by their parents. As working-class British youths delved more and more into these American forms, they began to identify not just with the music, but also with the white country musicians and black folk and blues musicians who had invented the genres.

The Who covered "Shakin' All Over" on their 1970 album, *Live at Leeds*.

Shakin' All Over

One British band that is little known in the United States anticipated the integration of R&B and rock 'n' roll that marked the British Invasion of 1964 and 1965. This group was Johnny Kidd and the Pirates, and it shaped many of the bands that emerged in the mid-'60s.

In 1959, Freddie Heath and the Nutters recorded Heath's song "Please Don't Touch." At the recording session, their record company told them that they would now be known as Johnny Kidd and the Pirates. As Kidd, Heath donned an eye patch and the band wore stylized pirate uniforms on stage and in their publicity photos.

Johnny Kidd and the Pirates' second single, "Shakin' All Over," cemented the importance of the band. This 1960 Kidd-penned song was the first British-composed rock song that was widely covered by bands around the world. From its melody, harmonic patterns and vocal and instrumental performance style, the original Johnny Kidd and the Pirates version of the song is a quintessential British take on American R&B.

The song became a hit in the United States in 1965 when it was covered by a Canadian band called Chad Allan and The Expressions. The record label, however, released it as a track by The Guess Who — hoping to create some buzz that maybe it was an anonymous release by one of the British Invasion bands, maybe even the Beatles themselves. Chad Allan and The Expressions were no more but still tour today as The Guess Who.

Actual British Invasion band The Who included "Shakin' All Over" in their classic 1970 album *Live at Leeds*. Legend has it that The Who added the song to their live shows because fans would confuse The Who and The Guess Who and expected to hear the song.

This was particularly true as the young Brits learned about the plight of blacks in the U.S. The disenfranchised British youths developed an affinity with American blacks in part because they, too, felt that they were members of an oppressed and marginalized group within their own society.

The English band Freddie and the Dreamers had a few hits in America in the mid 1960s.

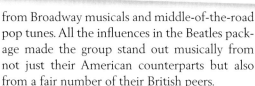

American blues musician Chuck Berry (below) was a major influence on the British Invasion, with many bands covering his songs, such as "Beautiful Delilah" by The Kinks (above) and "Reelin' and Rockin'" by The Dave Clark Five (right).

For some young working-class British musicians, the natural connection with African-American blues and R&B was so strong that by the end of the 1950s, some young Brits jumped directly into blues and R&B, bypassing skiffle as a gateway. By the early 1960s, the live and recorded repertoire of numerous British rock 'n' roll bands was heavily blues and R&B based, especially compared to white American rock 'n' roll bands. The Beatles performed and recorded Motown songs, 1950s rock 'n' rolls songs by black singer-songwriters such as Chuck Berry and Little Richard, and tunes written for black female vocal groups such as The Cookies.

The 1964 Explosion

The sense of loss that followed the assassination of President John F. Kennedy in November 1963, the Beatles' national television exposure on the *Ed Sullivan Show* and the hype heaped upon the Beatles by radio personalities such as New York's Murray the K all played a role in starting what became the British Invasion. But the importance of the music itself cannot be ignored. White American rock bands of the time simply had not integrated R&B, Motown and electric blues into their sound to the extent that the Beatles and other British bands had. The bands of the British Invasion were a sonic sea change from the crooners and folk singers that preceded them. Americans had few acts that could compete on these new terms.

To top it off, Paul McCartney and John Lennon, in particular, were writing songs that integrated the influences of R&B, folk revival, country and 1950s-style rock 'n' roll, along with their own personal touches. In addition, the Beatles had the audacity to cover songs from Broadway musicals and middle-of-the-road pop tunes. All the influences in the Beatles package made the group stand out musically from not just their American counterparts but also from a fair number of their British peers.

Just how great an impact did the Beatles and their counterparts make? In 1960 and 1961, no British artist hit No. 1 in the American pop charts. In 1962, two British instrumentals, "Stranger on the Shore" and "Telstar," made it to the top of the U.S. charts. Fast forward to 1964: In the first year of the British Invasion, nine of the 23 songs that topped the U.S. charts were by British artists, and six of those were Lennon-McCartney compositions recorded by the Beatles. By 1965, Peter and Gordon, Manfred Mann, Herman's Hermits, the Rolling Stones, The Dave Clark Five, Petula Clark, Wayne Fontana and the Mindbenders, the Animals, and Freddie and the Dreamers had all topped the U.S. record charts. In fact, in 1965, 12 of the year's 25 chart-toppers were by British artists, with the Beatles owning four of them. ◐

James E. Perone is a professor of music at the University of Mount Union in Ohio. He is the author of several books, including Mods, Rockers, and the Music of the British Invasion. *Because it sums up the band's philosophy and gives John, Paul, George and Ringo the chance to show off their instrumental chops, his favorite Beatles' track is "The End."*

The Wanna-Beatles

In the wake of the initial wave of Beatlemania, many other performers either sought to imitate the Beatles or were overtly assisted by them. In all sorts of ways — directly and indirectly, consciously and unconsciously — groups on both sides of the Atlantic betrayed the influence of the group from Liverpool.

For a while, the Beatles' mop-top haircut, or a close approximation of it, was an obligatory accessory for aspiring young British groups. The Beatles' success also confirmed the performance lineup of lead guitar, bass guitar, rhythm guitar and drums that was automatically adopted by the vast majority of musicians in Britain and America. And while few groups went to the lengths of the Grasshoppers or Erkey Grant & the Eerwigs in using a name that so closely echoed the insect connotations of the Beatles, there were many others who used names drawn from the animal kingdom — the Byrds, the Monkees, the Turtles.

Across the United States, the Beatles' distinctive Englishness was increasingly copied in the presentation of groups such as the Beau Brummels from San Francisco, the Knickerbockers from New Jersey and the Buckinghams from Chicago. The inclusion of Manchester-born Davy Jones in the Monkees was an astute move by the group's creators that gave their deliberate reproduction of the Beatles' individual personalities — John Lennon/Micky Dolenz, George Harrison/Mike Nesmith, Ringo Starr/Peter Tork, Paul McCartney/Davy Jones — an even greater commercial impact.

On occasion, the Beatles would willingly go out of their way to help the careers of some of their fellow musicians. In the mid-1960s, McCartney gave the song "World Without Love" to students Peter Asher (the brother of his girlfriend Jane Asher) and Gordon Waller. This signaled the start of a hugely successful recording career. As Peter and Gordon, the duo enjoyed a string of hit singles that included the Lennon-McCartney compositions "Nobody I Know," "I Don't Want To See You Again" and "Woman."

The Beatles' efforts to launch the career of Liverpool singer Tommy Quickly proved less successful. After his version of their song "Tip of My Tongue" unexpectedly failed to enter the charts, the group included him in several of their U.K. tours and contributed to his unreleased recording of "No Reply." An extensive campaign to promote the singer in Britain and America came to nothing, and Quickly soon became the forgotten man of Brian Epstein's stable. The same fate awaited The Strangers with Mike Shannon, who in addition to routinely appearing in the same collarless jackets worn by the Beatles, released Lennon-McCartney's "One and One Is Two," only to see it slip into obscurity.

Others, including Marmalade, Cliff Bennett and the Rebel Rousers, the Overlanders, and David and Jonathan, propelled themselves into the U.K. singles charts by releasing near-identical versions of Beatles' album tracks. And some established solo singers underwent abrupt changes of style. In the U.K., Adam Faith departed from the light, Buddy Holly-tinged pop that had brought him more than a dozen consecutive chart hits to record "The First Time" — a startlingly accurate reproduction of the Beatles' vocal and instrumental mannerisms. In America, Bobby Vee abandoned the double-tracked, orchestrally accompanied songs on which his career had been built to release an entire album called,

AP PHOTO

The U.K. duo Peter and Gordon recorded a few hit singles written and composed by Lennon and McCartney.

unashamedly, *Bobby Vee Sings The New Sound From England*. Tracks such as "She's Sorry" and "I'll Make You Mine" came complete with falsetto screams, "yeah, yeah" choruses and descending guitar chords.

At first, the Beatles were largely ambivalent about those who sought to copy them — as in any creative endeavor, imitation is the sincerest form of flattery. But as the size, scale and detail of the duplications expanded, their indifference turned into irritation. "It annoys me a lot ... why can't these copyists make their own styles like we did?" asked John Lennon in 1964.

— *Ian Inglis*

AP PHOTO / N

1963

1965

Come Together

John Lennon and Paul McCartney created the most successful songwriting partnership in history.

BY
GILLIAN G.
GAAR

In the great John Lennon vs. Paul McCartney debate, views usually split along stereotypical lines. John was the aggressive rocker; Paul the lightweight milquetoast. John was progressive; Paul was conventional. John bared his soul; Paul wrote silly love songs. The debate also has an underlying subtext: John, being dead, can be eulogized as a hero and martyr. Paul, still alive, can more easily serve as a guilt-free punching bag.

1968

This latter attitude was especially prevalent in the first years after Lennon's murder; people praising Lennon used that as an opportunity to knock McCartney. Whereas the question that should be asked is: why does it have to be John vs. Paul at all? It surely misses the point that the Beatles' success was due to it being John *and* Paul, each man as essential to the songwriting team as the other.

The polarized view of the two (John the hard man and Paul the softy) does have elements of truth, but it would be more accurate to characterize Lennon as being more impulsive and McCartney more cautious. McCartney made this assessment himself, telling Beatles biographer Hunter Davies, "I do stand back at times, unlike John … I don't like being the careful one. I'd rather be immediate like John. He was all action."

Lennon also agreed with this view of their relationship, pointing to how the lyrics of "We Can Work It Out" revealed their personalities: "You've got Paul writing *'we can work it out'* — y'know, real optimistic, and me, impatient: *'life is very short / and there's no time / for fussing and fighting my friend.'*"

Complementary and Competitive

However, what's often overlooked in the debate is that Lennon and McCartney's differences complemented each other; it's what made them such an unbeatable songwriting team in the first place. The natural push-pull of their relationship bolstered their strengths, and helped to check their weaknesses. It's also why their work in the Beatles is consistently stronger than their work as solo artists. The arc from "Love Me Do" in 1962 to "Strawberry Fields Forever" in 1966 is breathtaking; neither Lennon or McCartney made such a progression in their solo work.

The other key element is that the partnership was a highly competitive one. Though the two enjoyed working together (Paul: "Collaborating with another writer makes it twice as easy … The ricochet is a great thing"), the partnership wasn't

1957
The year that John and Paul wrote their first songs together: "Hello Little Girl" and "One After 909"

July 6, 1957
The day John Lennon and Paul McCartney meet

AP PHOTO

Paul McCartney, his girlfriend Jane Asher and John Lennon arrive in Greece in 1967. Paul is holding the hand of John's son, Julian.

always 50/50. Usually, one writer composed most of a song, taking it to his partner to help finish it; a general rule of thumb is that the lead singer is the dominant writer.

And despite the fact that the songwriting royalties were split 50/50, Lennon and McCartney would nonetheless vie to get their song as the A-side of the Beatles' singles, an indication of how important it was for each to be seen taking the lead.

This (mostly) friendly determination to one-up the other also meant that the Beatles' music was always progressing; neither Lennon or McCartney was interested in doing what they'd successfully accomplished before. And the pace at which Lennon and McCartney had to write (during 1963 alone, the Beatles released 19 Lennon-McCartney songs; seven other Lennon-McCartney songs that weren't recorded by the Beatles were also released by other artists) meant they spent a lot of time together perfecting their craft.

"They grew like hothouse plants," George Martin recalled. "They'd suddenly sprung up into writers of stature."

Influence on Each Other's Songs

Martin, who worked with the Beatles more than any other producer, was well placed to assess the Lennon-McCartney partnership. "Paul had a stronger sense of melody and harmony that appealed to the main mass of the public more," he told author Peter Du Noyer, "and John had a kookier way of dealing with lyrics, but they did influence each other enormously." Indeed, Lennon's love of word play attracted McCartney from the beginning; on first seeing Lennon perform live, he was amazed at how he sang the Del-Vikings' "Come and Go With Me" making up words on the spot, as he didn't know the lyrics.

It was Lennon's lyrical suggestion that gave McCartney's "I Saw Her Standing There" a more knowing edge. McCartney's opening couplet was "*She was just 17 / She'd never been a beauty queen.*" Lennon suggested changing the second line to the more suggestive "*You know what I mean.*"

What one might call his darker worldview also gave a different musical flavoring to "Michelle," when Lennon suggested the "*I love you, I love you*" passage for the bridge, inspired by Nina Simone's cover of Screaming Jay Hawkins' "I Put A Spell On You." "My contribution to Paul's songs was always to add a little bluesy edge to them," he explained. "Otherwise, y'know, 'Michelle' is a straight ballad, right? He provided a lightness, an optimism, while I would always go

"You'll Be Mine"

The first song credited to Lennon and McCartney that was recorded and officially released by the Beatles. The song was recorded in 1960 and included on *Anthology I* (released in 1995).

1968

for the sadness, the discords, the bluesy notes."

But McCartney could supply a bit of bite as well, not only suggesting the lines about "Norwegian Wood" in the song of the same name, but also providing the idea for the song's ending, where the protagonist burns down the house of the woman who spurned it, giving the number "a little sting in the tail," as McCartney put it. Always a more meticulous musician, Paul knew how to bring disparate song fragments together, as when he added the *"Woke up / fell out of bed"* sequence to Lennon's "A Day in the Life" or masterminded the medleys on side two of *Abbey Road*.

During the Beatles' later years, the two wrote together less frequently, as their songwriting styles began to diverge. The balance had also shifted; while John's was the dominant voice on the Beatles' pre-1966 singles, McCartney came to the fore post-1966. There were still occasional collaborations — as when McCartney's verses in "I've Got a Feeling" were nicely counterpointed by Lennon's *Everybody had a hard time* sequence during the song's bridge — but each man was now more inclined to go his own way.

But what a rich and varied body of work Lennon and McCartney left behind. And so committed were they to the songwriting partnership that they credited each other on every song they wrote no matter how much either

had contributed to it — John even used the credit Lennon-McCartney on his first solo single, "Give Peace a Chance" (though Paul would later have an issue with the name order of "Lennon-McCartney"). That each man could fully appreciate what the other brought to the table helped make John Lennon and Paul McCartney an unbeatable songwriting team. ◯

Summer of 1963

The first tune penned by Lennon-McCartney hits the U.S. charts. It's Del Shannon's version of "From me to You."

1969

The last time the Beatles recorded a song together. The song, appropriately called, "The End," was written by Paul and ends with a couplet that McCartney said was inspired by Shakespeare:

"And in the end the love you take Is equal to the love you make."

Let Me Take You Down

John Lennon and "Strawberry Fields Forever" showcase how art was born from crisis.

The Beatles produced some of their most adventurous work in 1966. The year also marked the greatest crisis they had experienced since skulking away from Hamburg in late 1960. The band's meteoric rise had plateaued in early '66 when hopes for a third feature film and a companion recording project in the U.S. were abandoned. *Revolver* — rated by many as the greatest pop album of all time — put them back on track, but devastating new lows arrived with the year's world tour.

BY WALTER EVERETT

IMAGINE

In New York's Central Park, a 2.5-acre section of the park was named "Strawberry Fields" on Oct. 9, 1985 (on what would have been Lennon's 45th birthday) and features the Imagine memorial (above). In 1966, Beatles fans protested over Lennon's remark that the band was more popular than Jesus (left). John spent that fall in Europe (at left, he and wife Cynthia return to London from Spain) where he wrote "Strawberry Fields Forever."

GUNTER ZINT / PICTURE-ALLIANCE/AP IMAGES

AP PHOTO

Amid protests over his comments about Jesus, John Lennon went to Germany in 1966 to film the movie *How I Won the War* which was directed by John Lester (pictured with Lennon above).

■ John Lennon opened the U.S. leg of the tour with a confused and humiliating apology for statements he had made comparing the Beatles to Christ. This was just seven weeks after an American album cover was declared tasteless by retailers and withdrawn in an unprecedented retreat. (Known now as the "butcher" cover, the *Yesterday and Today* album featured the Beatles in white smocks holding pieces of meat and doll parts.)

■ Rigid confinement by armed guards over three full days in Tokyo was followed by a capricious and dangerous lack of security in Manila.

■ Appearances in the American South were occasions for record burnings, Klan protests and death threats.

These hardships and backlashes punctuated a dismal tour. The band's under-rehearsed approach to complex music, that remained inaudible anyway, rendered performances profoundly dissatisfying, and the stadiums were undersold, to boot. After the last concert on Aug. 29, 1966, George Harrison proclaimed, "Well, that's it; I'm not a Beatle anymore."

Separation in the Fall of 1966

Instead of regrouping in London to record an album for the Christmas market, as they had done every year after 1962, the four Beatles dispersed to the world's four corners. Paul McCartney spent the fall of '66 on safari in Kenya and wrote the soundtrack for *The Family Way* — the first music to be credited to a solo Beatle. Lennon had a film role, acting in *How I Won the War*, which was shot in Germany and Spain that September

through November. Harrison studied sitar under Ravi Shankar in Bombay and toured the subcontinent. Ringo Starr caught up with family at home in Surrey.

Lennon was particularly at odds with himself as he sat in Spain, dreaming of his material and spiritual home, contemplating how his defining traits were perceived by himself, by his suddenly distant partners and by others.

Because Lennon used his art as an emotional release — as he acknowledged doing in "I'm a Loser" and "Help!" for instance — we can imagine that the deep identity crisis that overtook him in the fall of 1966 brought him to a similarly productive catharsis as he picked up a nylon-string classical guitar in seaside Almería, considered some of the emotional trials he had endured at different points in his life and began composing "Strawberry Fields Forever." As Lennon said, "'Strawberry Fields' was psychoanalysis set to music, really."

When this song was released with "Penny Lane" in February 1967 as a double A-side single, Beatles' fans were mystified. They were slow to accept the band's radical facial hair and unconventional clothing, an inscrutable baroque surface under which peculiar fantasies played.

The films promoting the two sides of the new single were bizarre. Other puzzles surrounded whatever meanings might lie behind the four toddlers' snapshots (the Beatles' own) on the single's picture sleeve and the perplexing aerial photo of the suburban Penny Lane district of Liverpool that appeared in teaser ads for the new disc. The listening public struggled to understand that the Beatles were attempting new poetic ex-

Strawberry Field

Strawberry Field was a Salvation Army home right around the corner from where John lived with his Aunt Mimi. Abandoned by both parents when he was very young, John could identify with the neighborhood orphans as he attended their annual summer fundraising fair or played in their trees just a leap over the wall.

The orphanage is now long gone, but Yoko's Strawberry Fields memorial to John sits in Central Park in New York, directly across from the Dakota building where John and Yoko lived for his final seven years. The Dakota's tall, carved-stone gables and arched window surrounds are eerily reminiscent of the building that housed Strawberry Field.

pressions of a return to blissful innocence.

We don't know what led Paul to create a companion piece to John's new offering, but we are given two Liverpool odes that complement each other well. McCartney's Edenic "Penny Lane" is graced with direct, representational lyrics featuring quaint characters who played within a clearly drawn picture: the barber, the banker, the fireman and the nurse all make sense to the listener.

The Meaning Behind Strawberry Fields

"Strawberry Fields Forever," on the other hand, is an indecipherable, impressionistic jumble of images vaguely evocative of misunderstanding, insecurities and indifference — all somehow tied to a land of trees and fields.

It's partly the indirect mode with which Lennon recalls his childhood and considers a lifelong otherness that plants his fantasy at artistic depths. *"Nothing is real and nothing to get hung about / it's getting hard to be someone / it doesn't matter much to me / that is, you can't, you know, tune in but it's all right"* — these and other lines express a fluid identity, an insecurity in one's surroundings, an inability to make himself understood by others and a detachment from the everyday.

The words are intentionally loose, controversial and anti-poetic. They speak directly but resist clarity. The song's complexity and its indirectness suggest a defensive mechanism that

> "The second line goes, *'No one I think is in my tree.'* Well, what I was trying to say ... in my insecure way, is **'Nobody seems to understand where I'm coming from**.*'*"
>
> — *Interview with* Playboy, *1980*

buffers the pain brought by eruptions of lifelong negative memories.

The song's musical factors, like its lyrics, convey a vague and wondrous misfittedness. Paul's Mellotron intro articulates flute samples made alien by trimming away their sonic attacks and decays. Lennon's ambivalent chords portray the elusiveness of goals through pitch alterations and motions forward then backward in relation to stable tonal reference points. An abrupt jump from guitars and keyboards to cellos and trumpets thwarts the listener's attempt to find secure grounding. Timbre-distorting tape speeds and intermittent backward percussion transport the singer and listener deep into the past, perhaps to a time preceding exile.

"Strawberry Fields Forever" was released to waves of misunderstanding and awe, the composer's psyche center stage but buried under cryptic armor — a pose revisited in "I Am the Walrus," "Glass Onion" and "Come Together."

In the years since John died, the song's reputation has grown. It's a shining example of the Beatles' artistry and their commitment to searching for human understanding and transcendence. ◖

Walter Everett is a professor at the University of Michigan and the author of the two-volume set The Beatles as Musicians. *He is unable to name a single favorite Beatles song, but believes that "Strawberry Fields Forever" may be their most significant recording.*

Although the Salvation Army home is gone, the gates at Strawberry Field in Woolton, a suburb of Liverpool, still stand.

Breaching the Iron

The Beatles were the ultimate symbol of freedom in communist countries.

BY ALI LITTMAN

In 1962, Nikita Khrushchev declared the electric guitar an "enemy of the people." Two years later, teenagers in the U.S.S.R. were secretly making their own electric guitars to impersonate a new, beloved band — the Beatles. The Fab Four captivated young people behind the Iron Curtain, but it wasn't easy to love the fun-loving band. The Beatles were banned in the U.S.S.R., and it wouldn't be until 1986 that a complete Beatles album would be released there. Despite efforts to eradicate Beatlemania, the government was no match for the ardent Beatles fans in the Soviet Union.

"It was illegal.
If something [is] illegal,
people want it more and more.
It means a piece of freedom."
— Vova Katzman, owner of the Kavern in Kiev

Curtain

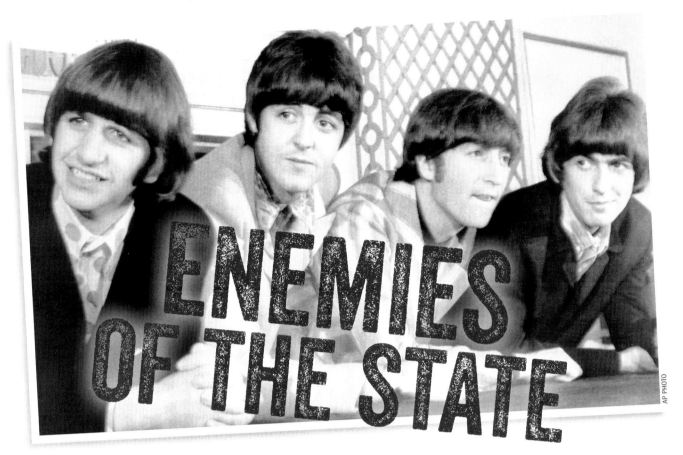

ENEMIES OF THE STATE

While the Beatles weren't the first rock band whose music had reached the Soviet Union, they gripped young people's hearts like no other band had before. Beatles music contained everything young people felt was lacking — joy, spontaneity, beauty and rhythm, according to Art Troitsky, one of the most prominent rock journalists in Russia, in an interview in Leslie Woodhead's *How The Beatles Rocked The Kremlin*.

The Beatles Black Market

Beatles' music made its way into the U.S.S.R. through albums smuggled in from abroad or music played on foreign radio stations with powerful enough signals to beam into the Soviet Union. When Soviet authorities noticed the Beatles' burgeoning popularity, they jammed foreign radio stations, instructed censors to destroy any Beatles' records, and spread anti-Beatles propaganda.

One cartoon published in the Soviet Union called the Beatles "The Bugs" and depicted insect poison being poured over the scuttling Beatles. An article in the Soviet newspaper *Pravda* said the Beatles sat on the toilet in their raincoats to perform. A bizarre propaganda film claimed that the Beatles got their start performing in swimming trunks with toilet seats around their necks.

The government had reason to put down the Beatles. Soviet youth had been raised to view the West as their enemy. When the Beatles showed up, young people realized that something wasn't quite right about that viewpoint, according to Sasha Lipnitsky of the Russian rock band Zvuki Mu.

In order to foster their love for the forbidden band, Beatles fans resorted to developing a network of underground markets, bands and concerts. The black market boasted an array of Beatles paraphernalia, including albums made out of discarded X-ray plates. Known as "ribs," these albums were widely available and could be bought for practically nothing. Fans and entrepreneurs made the X-ray discs by cutting a hole in the middle of the image, rounding the sides with scissors, and recording music onto the X-ray with a modified record player. These improvised records were flexible, meaning they could be hidden up a coat sleeve. The fact that the latest Beatles record was embossed on an X-ray of a skull or femur did nothing to diminish its appeal.

In its attempts to stop the spread of these records, the government flooded the streets with counterfeit copies that spit insults at the listeners, calling them anti-Soviet slime. When tape recorders became widely available, fans recorded LPs on tapes, selling them on the black market, too. Fans also took pictures of photos of the band to sell at underground markets. Some photos were even rented out so fans could enjoy them for a short period of time. Another pastime, according to Woodhead, included swapping Beatles memorabilia.

Imitators Great and Small

Beatles' fans knew it would be a long time, if ever, before they saw the Beatles perform live. So, they created the next best thing — cover bands. According to Woodhead, "There was not a band anywhere in the Soviet Union that did not start life as a Beatles tribute band."

Andrew Makarevich, founder of the famous Russian rock band Time Machine, says that from the moment he heard the Beatles he knew he wanted to be like them. First, however, he had to find a suitable electric guitar, which at the time, wasn't for sale in the U.S.S.R. Buying a piece of wood and painting it red, Makarevich tried to recreate Lennon's guitar. But, he was stuck when he realized he needed a pickup, a device that converts guitar strums into electrical signals. When Makarevich heard that a pickup could be made from public telephone handsets, he stole the necessary parts and made his first electric guitar.

Makarevich's band began playing in underground concerts. The only way to find out about an underground concert was by word of mouth because the venues were absolutely secret. A concert organizer could be arrested for "breaching social order," especially if tickets were sold — which would mean the organizer was working on the black market.

Time Machine soon turned into a full-fledged rock band, writing and performing its own songs for its own fan base. The story is the same for hundreds of bands across the U.S.S.R. that all got their starts as Beatles impersonators.

Realizing they were fighting a losing battle, the state published its first positive article on the Beatles in 1968 in the magazine, *Musical Life*. The government even created its own robotic-sounding rock band known as the Happy Guys. They played Beatles songs, including "Ob-La-Di, Ob-La-Da." The Happy Guys' other songs praised socialism and encouraged young people to look forward to a socialist future.

The Communist Bloc and Beyond

In Soviet satellite countries outside the U.S.S.R., official policies toward rock music and the Beatles varied, while fans possessed the same fervent love for the band. In 1964 a local Czech journalist (as described in Sabrina Ramet's book *Rocking the State*) reported on Beatlemania there: "They wriggled, they fell off the platform and crawled back onto it, they gasped for air hysterically. I expected them to bite each other any minute. And then the destruction began." Fans rushed the stage, seizing chairs, chucking them across the room and breaking windows. Beatlemania — even with Beatles cover bands — had spread, striking fear in satellite governments as it had in the U.S.S.R.

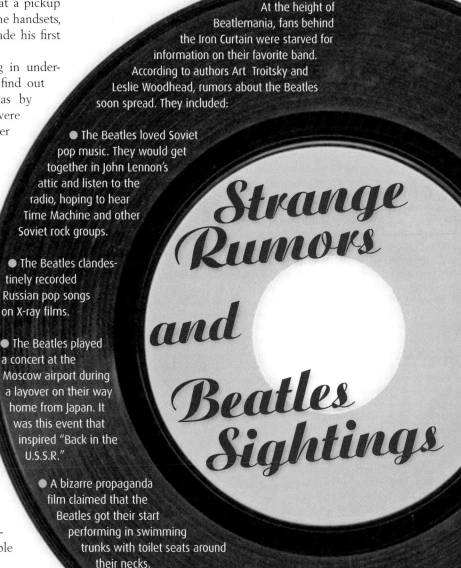

At the height of Beatlemania, fans behind the Iron Curtain were starved for information on their favorite band. According to authors Art Troitsky and Leslie Woodhead, rumors about the Beatles soon spread. They included:

● The Beatles loved Soviet pop music. They would get together in John Lennon's attic and listen to the radio, hoping to hear Time Machine and other Soviet rock groups.

● The Beatles clandestinely recorded Russian pop songs on X-ray films.

● The Beatles played a concert at the Moscow airport during a layover on their way home from Japan. It was this event that inspired "Back in the U.S.S.R."

● A bizarre propaganda film claimed that the Beatles got their start performing in swimming trunks with toilet seats around their necks.

Strange Rumors and Beatles Sightings

REX FEATURES VIA AP IMAGES

In East Germany, concerts, discos, radio stations and television stations were mandated to maintain a 60:40 ratio in which 60 percent of music had to be from socialist countries while 40 percent could be from other countries. When John Lennon died, a newspaper in East Germany saw it as an opportunity to spread anti-American propaganda, printing the headline "Singer John Lennon Just One of 21,000 Murder Victims Annually (in the U.S.)."

Meanwhile, fans behind the Iron Curtain mourned with the rest of the world. Radio Sofia in Bulgaria saluted Lennon's death in a two-hour tribute. In Czechoslovakia, fans erected shrines for Lennon and decorated a wall next to the Charles Bridge in honor of the fallen Beatle. The wall still stands today.

By the mid-1970s in the U.S.S.R., rules on rock music relaxed slightly as relations between the East and West improved. In 1977, the government allowed state record stores to sell *Band on the Run* by Wings, though it would still be nine years until a complete Beatles' album would be sold in the U.S.S.R.

In 1979, Elton John was permitted to perform a series of nine concerts in the U.S.S.R. By no means was John to play "Back in the U.S.S.R.," the government instructed. Officials deemed the song too sensitive, and for the first eight concerts,

Ringo Starr was the first Beatle to visit the U.S.S.R. in 1998. He played there again in 2011 (above). In 1979, Elton John made headlines when he played nine concerts in the U.S.S.R. At left, he tours the Krelim with his mother and stepfather, Sheila and Fred Farebrother.

AP PHOTO / BORIS YURCHENKO

John abided by their wishes. On the ninth concert, however, John jammed out to the forbidden song, "Back in the U.S.S.R." Young people attending the concert, who had been forced to sit in the very back of the hall, burst forward cheering, stomping past Soviet officials.

It would only be a matter of time before a Beatles' fan would come to power in the U.S.S.R. That person was Mikhail Gorbachev. Under his leadership, the first full Beatles' album, *A Hard Day's Night*, was finally released in the U.S.S.R. in 1986. A year later, Gorbachev and his wife, Raisa, received Yoko Ono in Moscow.

The first Beatle stepped foot in the U.S.S.R. in 1998 when Ringo Starr played to a packed hall in Moscow. "It would have been nice if we could have come a bit earlier, but I tell you it's better late than never," Starr told the crowd.

Paul McCartney finally made his way to the U.S.S.R. in 2003, playing a legendary concert in Red Square to 20,000 people, including Vladimir Putin. As McCartney sang "Back in the U.S.S.R.," people cheered, danced, laughed, cried and sang along to that Beatles' anthem, forbidden in the U.S.S.R. for more than 30 years. ◉

Ali Littman is an author living in Washington, D.C. She is currently working on her first novel. Her favorite Beatles' song is "Hey Jude."

In 2003, Paul McCartney performed at Red Square to 20,000 screaming fans.

AP PHOTO / IVAN SEKRETAREV

SHUTTERSTOCK / PETER SCHOLZ

In Paul McCartney's book, *Each One Believing: On Stage, Off Stage, and Backstage*, he recalls meeting former Soviet leader Mikhail Gorbachev, who told him through a translator that "the Beatles' music has taught the young people of the Soviet Union that there is another life. That there is freedom elsewhere, and, of course, this feeling has pushed them toward *perestroika*, toward the dialogue with the outside world."

President Vladimir Putin, who attended McCartney's 2003 concert, told him that the Beatles' music "was like a gulp of freedom" when he was young.

DEBATE:

The Fab Four's

Fab 5

Two music critics try to find the Beatles top five songs.

BY
PATRICK
FOSTER
AND
TIM
RILEY

Let us proclaim first off what an arbitrary and pleasantly unpredictable process picking 20 Beatles favorites proves, never mind a top five. It makes for a fiendishly tempting way to argue about things. Ask us next year — or even next month — and this list might wind up composed of entirely different songs, such is the grandeur of this catalog. Our only goal was to spread selections across the Beatles' early, middle and late years.

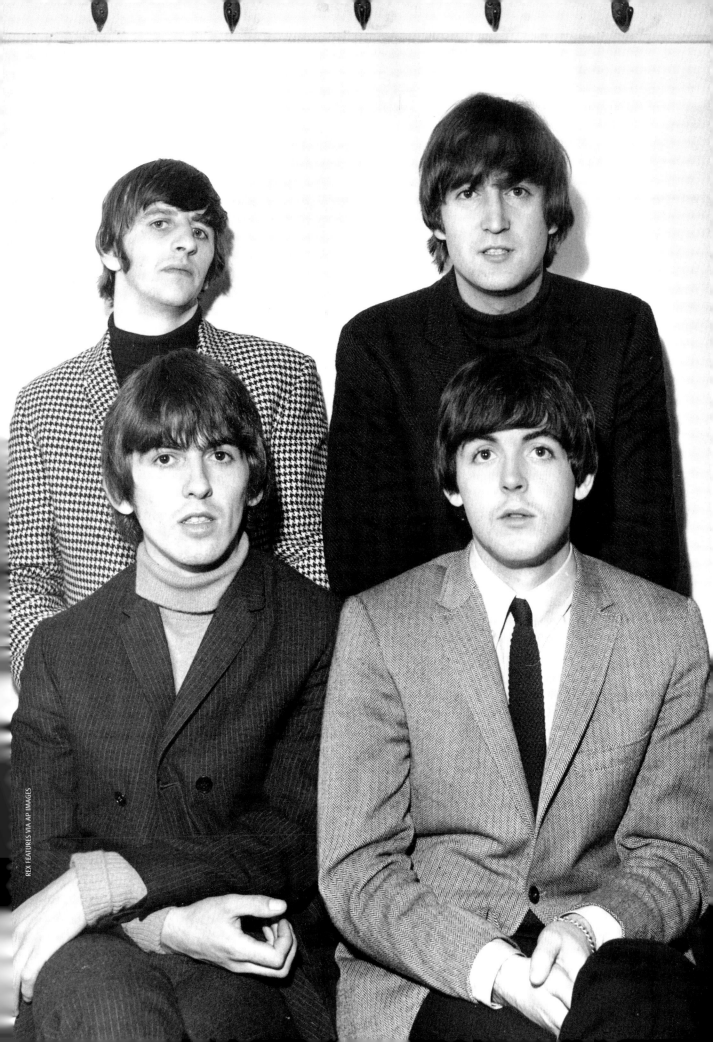

Tim: "Revolution No. 9" from *The Beatles (The White Album)*

I pick this song both for its disorienting contours as music concrète (found sound alongside melody and harmony) and alien status as a Lennon-McCartney non-sing-along. Like "A Day In the Life" and "Tomorrow Never Knows," it casts a long shadow across its album, and its perversity gives everything else poise — as if "Cry Baby Cry" had gently hypnotized side four of *The White Album* off into dreamland. Inside this experimental track's meandering compartments, the radio wonderland of Lennon's deep psyche peeks through. Feint cries of Beatlemania echo in its chambers. With hindsight, you have to wonder why Lennon had to fight for its inclusion while McCartney didn't have to mount any argument for "Honey Pie."

The Beatles at a press conference in August 1964 in New York during their first concert tour in the U.S.

Patrick: "She Said, She Said" from *Revolver*

I won't be able to get "number nine, number nine" out of my head for a week (but I appreciate the choice). I'm going with the final track on side one of *Revolver* (I have a theory about the best song on any album being the last song on side one, but that's another topic).

While the band had been heavy and powerful before, nothing they had committed to tape was as lush, powerful and as lyrically mind-slapping as this otherworldly Lennon track. There are lots of stories about the origins of its lyrics (*"She said, I know what it likes to be dead"* was supposedly inspired by Peter Fonda's stoned musings), but it's velvety hammer bass, gut-grabbing guitar and drums that toss you around like a dinghy on a stormy sea are what really matter. Lennon's talismanic vocal — which floats above and around and across and really seems like it has seen the other side (and been spooked by it) — ices this delicious 2:37 slice of cake.

AP PHOTO

Who are the Critics?

Tim Riley has written *Tell Me Why: A Beatles Commentary* and *Lennon: Man, Myth, Music*, among other books. He teaches journalism at Emerson College in Boston.

Patrick Foster works on digital media projects for *USA Today* and writes about music for a variety of publications. He sometimes plays guitar and yells for a band called Wingtip Sloat.

Tim: "That Means A Lot" from *Anthology 2*

Patrick, you stole my track!

For me the best tracks gravitate toward the end of side two, so I like the way you turn album sequences inside out.

I first heard "That Means a Lot" on a bootleg in the late 1980s, and it rang out like the ultimate throwaway only a great band might have the confidence to discard (it finally appeared on *Anthology 2*).

To my ear, McCartney the musician ranks as follows: He's first a bassist ("Rain," "Don't Let Me Down," "Something"), then a singer ("Long Tall Sally," "I'm Down," "Got To Get You Into My Life") and then a songwriter, with pros and cons that rub hard against one another. His melodies can soar even when cloyingly sung ("Eleanor Rigby," "Here, There and Everywhere"), and his coyness annoys even when framed by tart arrangements ("For No One," "When I'm Sixty Four," "Martha My Dear").

This early 1965 track (left off the *Help!* soundtrack) finds his sweet spot, alongside "You Won't See Me," "For No One," "Penny Lane," and "Get Back." Screaming *"Can't you see?!"* into the fadeout, he sounds like he's warming up for "Hey Jude." The Spector-esque production veils but doesn't mask a deeply erotic anger. And the lyric resists romantic cliché by circling that rarest of McCartney themes: humility.

Patrick: "Everybody's Got Something to Hide (Except for Me and My Monkey)" from *The Beatles (The White Album)*

Tim, that's a great choice — Beatles fans who haven't heard it should find it right now!

The first few times I heard *The White Album*, I wasn't particularly impressed. (I'll admit I was much more into The Clash and Black Flag at the time). One evening about a few years later, I was at a friend's house and he was playing an old Warner Brother's compilation record that contained Fats Domino covering "Everybody's Got Something to Hide." I was surprised and delighted by his loosely swinging version and made a note to go back and listen to the original a little more closely.

Not only did this cause me to reevaluate my stance on *The White Album*, but it sparked a personal Beatles revival. And it was this frantic, scrambling track that led the way. (That enigmatic indie rockers The Feelies covered it on their debut album didn't hurt, either.)

With its emphasis on stereo separation and stutter-step intro that lurches forward into a headlong charge, this Lennon-penned rocker emphasizes feel over message and impact over everything else. The bell that rings incessantly in the left channel adds an element of hysteria that is whipped into shape by the lacerating guitar breaks in the chorus. And so what if the words are basically nonsense? The "whooooo!" that erupts at :39 is, in my view, the skin-tingling moment of the band's late-period.

In 1965, the Beatles — still sporting "mop tops"— released *Help!* and *Rubber Soul.*

PRNEWSFOTO / APPLE CORPS LTD. / EMI MUSIC

USA Today's Elysa Gardner chose "Ticket to Ride" as the Beatles' best song:

"No single better reflects the mix of ambition, tension and pure pop genius that made the Beatles unique."

Tim: "Happiness is a Warm Gun" from *The Beatles (The White Album)*

Patrick, you stole my track again! Literally next up on my list was the thunderous "Monkey," so you force my hand: I choose "Happiness is a Warm Gun," its tricky cousin, which falls ... at the end of side one (dun dun DUN).

"Monkey" is a tart, mangled, screwball farce. Having been maneuvered into this corner, I choose its polar opposite, the maniacal rant of a lecherous junkie in his *"multi-colored mirrors on his hobnail boots,"* whose *"hands are busy working overtime,"* who climaxes with a magnificent doo-wop coda as the junk hits his veins. Those *"Mother superiors"* are a nice touch!

This song finds Lennon rediscovering the blues after jumping off experimental ledges with "Tomorrow Never Knows," "A Day in the Life" and "I Am the Walrus." The track sits alongside other late songs with stabbing vocals inside traditional frames like "Yer Blues," "I Want You (She's So Heavy)" and "Don't Let Me Down."

Like "Monkey," "Happiness" reaches extreme ensemble funk: As the band falls apart, it still summons intricacy and precise timing around sharp rhythmic curves. Inside a narrative of stray insights, acute observations and lickety-split reversals, comes a mangy guitar solo, spewing degenerate glamor to embarrass the candid junkie lyrics.

Whoops, that makes two on my list off the overrated *The White Album*. What can I say? You inspire me.

Patrick: "Please Please Me" from *Please Please Me*

One of the great things about the Beatles is the incredibly rich amount of historical material available to fans. And I must admit, I absolutely love being able to re-live, through reading and listening, the magic of Beatlemania.

I'm especially enamored of the moment when, after the band completed the final take of this song on Nov. 26, 1962, producer George Martin pressed the control room intercom and calmly announced, "Congratulations, gentlemen, you've just made your first No. 1." (And he was right, sort of — the single peaked at No. 2.)

The record's steady march up the U.K. charts unleashed the first wave of Beatles' adulation across England and prompted Martin to call the band off of a tour to record their first full-length album. Which they did ... in one day, before heading back out on the road.

Aside from its historical significance, the song itself is a raw, refreshing blast of unvarnished guitar — including a memorable, ringing figure played by George Harrison — and thrilling harmonies.

As has been pointed out by astute critics (most notably Ian MacDonald in his seminal *Revolution in the Head*), the record's main influence is the Everly Brothers' 1960 hit "Cathy's Clown," one of the very best records ever made by anyone anywhere.

AP PHOTO

Tim: "If I Fell" from
A Hard Day's Night

Lennon sings the preamble, peering over a ledge between commitment and reluctance, and the song spins out indecision through intricate vocal harmonies. For the verses, McCartney's upper line ducks and glides with geometric lyricism, often in the opposite direction to Lennon's vocals. Each individual line would have made a sturdy melody on its own; combined they trace a poetry of uncertainty. The lyrics describe love's oscillating, intemperate swells, seeking comfort and reassurance where only risk abides.

Was a ballad ever so fluid yet tough-minded? Would two writers harmonizing ever sound as timidly poised?

Patrick: "Come Together" from
Abbey Road

The opening salvo on *Abbey Road* was one of Lennon's two — with the grimy, addictive "I Want You (She's So Heavy)" — counterweights to McCartney's majestic swan-song medley on side two.

The world of indie rock in the mid-1980s to early 1990s was a wonderful place. We valued (okay, worshipped) strange strings of words, subversive little verbal tricks and raw, authentic sounding drums and guitars. "Come Together" overflows with all of those attributes and then some — from the unsettling and evocative images (*"spinal cracker," "mojo filter," "joo-joo eyeball,"* and how the heck do you *"shoot Coca-Cola?"*) to the warming-up-to-stomp-your-head-in drumming and paint-scraper guitar.

Best of all of course, is Lennon's whispered/shouted *"Shoot me!"* — which was mixed to lessen the shock into something that sounds like "shooook!" — that punctuates each creeping figure. In many ways, "Come Together" is a perfect indie-rock song.

That "Come Together" foreshadows Lennon's first wave of solo hits — "Power to the People" and others — is icing on the cake. And years later, when I actually listened closely to Chuck Berry's "You Can't Catch Me," the tune that is kissing cousins with "Come Together?" Chills, man.

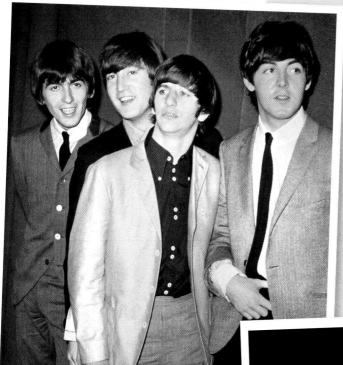

Not only did the look of the Fab Four evolve, their music did, too. The Beatles went from young lads (above in 1964) singing "yeah, yeah, yeah" to hippies (left in 1968 and right in 1969) writing about angst and playing more complex arrangements.

Tim: "Don't Let Me Down," the B-side to "Get Back"

Okay, confession: It fell down to a very hard choice between "Don't Let Me Down" and "A Day in the Life." Both have that collaborative spark and are duets. But "A Day in the Life" seems so obvious, right? That track still works its voodoo on classic rock radio, and in a weird way has aged less ironically than its themes deserve.

Perched on the tipping point of the Lennon-McCartney feud, this tune finds them sounding more like brothers than they have since "If I Fell" and climaxes a series of musical farewells they offered up in their final months together ("Two of Us," "I've Got a Feeling" and "I Dig a Pony").

Amid so many great late Lennon vocals, this exasperated exhortation still rings out as poetically as anything he ever did, including much of his work with the Plastic Ono Band. It's the one Beatles track where McCartney's upper harmony floats invisibly — most listeners don't even hear it as a duet. At the same time, McCartney's bass line descends stepwise beneath the bridge (*"I'm in love for the first time …"*) for an exquisite counterpoint. McCartney literally coddles Lennon from above and below.

The more you know about Beatles history, the more confounding "Don't Let Me Down" gets. Just who is Lennon addressing in this first-person narrative: Yoko Ono? Paul McCartney? The band dissolving beneath his yowls? Apple Corps on whose rooftop he sang the song for the *Let It Be* film? The rest of us?

In the weeks after his assassination in 1980, this track became as hard to listen to as that line in "The Ballad of John and Yoko" — *"The way things are going / They're gonna crucify me."*

Patrick: "Rain," the B-side to "Paperback Writer"

I was certain that we would land on the same top pick, Tim, but you went for their beautiful, bittersweet swan song. You are a true Beatles scholar. With my No. 1, I went for sheer sonic weight, sensory impact and personal connection — along with a bit of record-collector geekiness.

"Rain" is simply the Beatles song that hits me hardest, sonically and personally. Anyone who has ever been in a band (no matter how good or bad) gets a special thrill when playing a cover version of a song from a band they love, especially when it sounds at least halfway passable. Strumming the alternating C and G majors in "Rain" — drums crashing and bass rising and falling around you — is an incredibly empowering feeling. In the tiniest way, you feel more connected to your heroes.

The rush and buzz of something so simple but powerful inspires the urge to write and create and release records in a mad rush. That, for me, is what rock music is really about.

Lennon, of course, knew all those feelings by the time "Rain" was written and recorded. But he was also in the grip of something else.

Much has been written about "Rain" as a metaphor for (and attempt to express the sheer brain- and chest-pressing weight of) an LSD trip. And while the record itself is brilliantly recorded, taking the band into luminous sonic territory where every sound does indeed seem to glow from the inside, "Rain" also captures the band's musicianship at an absolute peak.

Starr has never been more rhythmically perfect, Harrison's leads whoosh, and McCartney is brilliant beyond comprehension — one could make an argument that his bassline here is the greatest in rock 'n' roll history. The harmonies show how closely the group was paying attention to the Beach Boys, while Lennon's keening, sneering vocal leaps out at the listener and asks, *"Are you with us, brother?"*

As a lifelong recording-collecting nerd, how could I not choose a B-side as my No. 1 song from the greatest rock band of all time? **O**

AP PHOTO

The trend-setting Beatles — performing in 1966 (left) and attending a lecture by Maharishi Mahesh Yogi in 1967.

Tim's Top 20

1. Don't Let Me Down
2. If I Fell
3. Happiness Is A Warm Gun
4. That Means a Lot
5. Revolution #9
6. You Won't See Me
7. I Saw Her Standing There
8. Rain
9. Dr. Robert
10. And Your Bird Can Sing
11. Strawberry Fields Forever
12. Penny Lane
13. Hey Jude
14. Revolution
15. I Should Have Known Better
16. Dear Prudence
17. Everybody's Got Something to Hide (Except for Me and My Monkey)
18. I Call Your Name
19. Sexy Sadie
20. You Know My Name (Look Up The Number)

Patrick's Top 20

1. Rain
2. Come Together
3. Please Please Me
4. Everybody's Got Something to Hide (Except for Me and My Monkey)
5. She Said, She Said
6. Dr. Robert
7. Twist and Shout
8. Paperback Writer
9. I Want to Hold Your Hand
10. I've Just Seen a Face
11. Happiness Is A Warm Gun
12. Taxman
13. Sun King/Mean Mr. Mustard
14. I Am the Walrus
15. Tomorrow Never Knows
16. Strawberry Fields Forever
17. Don't Let Me Down
18. A Hard Day's Night
19. The Ballad of John and Yoko
20. Back In the USSR

AP PHOTO

In 2004 *Rolling Stone* declared

"A Day in the Life"

from *Sgt. Pepper's* the Beatles' top song, writing, "In truth, the song was far too intense musically and emotionally for regular radio play. It wasn't really until the '80s, after Lennon's murder, that 'A Day in the Life' became recognized as the

band's masterwork.

In this song, as in so many other ways, the Beatles were way ahead of everyone else."

We
CAN'T
Work It Out

As ex-Beatles, John, Paul, George and Ringo saw their careers soar, stall and take strange turns.

The Beatles' breakup didn't happen overnight. The four Beatles grew apart personally and musically over a period of several years. The closest thing to an official announcement occurred on April 10, 1970, when Paul McCartney, promoting his first solo album, said that he did not foresee writing with John Lennon again. By then each had a distinct musical identity. Still young men — the Beatles were in their late 20s at the time of Paul's statement — they proceeded to create solo albums at a blistering pace. By the end of 1973, the ex-Beatles had accounted for 14 studio albums since the band's breakup. As the years passed and their output slowed, the ex-Beatles found other interests in art, politics and business. A reunion never appeared to have been seriously considered. John died in 1980; George in 2001.

BY
ARWEN
BICKNELL

In 1967, the Beatles had enjoyed three years of widespread popularity in the U.S. It would be another three years before the band broke up, with the Fab Four pursuing solo careers.

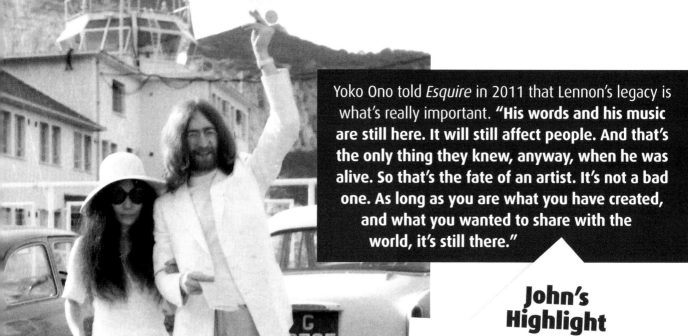

Yoko Ono told *Esquire* in 2011 that Lennon's legacy is what's really important. **"His words and his music are still here. It will still affect people. And that's the only thing they knew, anyway, when he was alive. So that's the fate of an artist. It's not a bad one. As long as you are what you have created, and what you wanted to share with the world, it's still there."**

Lennon and Ono's 1969 wedding at the Rock of Gibralter (above). John in 1980 (below), one month before his murder.

John's Highlight

Few would argue that the high point of Lennon's solo career — and his most lasting legacy — is the song "Imagine." It's his best-selling, best-remembered single, named by BMI as one of the 100 most-performed songs of the 20th century. Lennon himself mentioned it as one of the songs he was proudest of in a 1980 *Playboy* interview: "'Imagine,' 'Love' and those Plastic Ono Band songs stand up to any song that was written when I was a Beatle. Now, it may take you 20 or 30 years to appreciate that, but the fact is, if you check those songs out, you will see that it is as good as any [expletive] stuff that was ever done." While there is something a tad hypocritical about "a millionaire who said 'Imagine no possessions,'" as Elvis Costello pointed out in "The Other Side of Summer," it has nonetheless become a revered anthem of world unity for three generations.

John's Lowlight

Some Time in New York City, Lennon's 1972 album, marked an artistic low point — *Rolling Stone* said, "The tunes are shallow and derivative and the words little more than sloppy nursery rhymes" — but Lennon's ugly attacks on Paul McCartney are the most noteworthy low. McCartney was hardly blameless, attacking his ex-partner in his own lyrics, but Lennon responded with twice the vitriol. In "How Do You Sleep?" Lennon sang, *"The only thing you done was yesterday,"* and *"The sound you make is muzak to my ears."* Ironically, this track was on Lennon's *Imagine* album — proving that "a brotherhood of man" is no easy thing.

John Lennon

After the breakup of the band, Lennon was the Beatle most associated with political and lifestyle activism. "Give Peace a Chance" — released before the breakup — became an anthem of the anti-war movement, and John, in his lyrics and actions, seemed intent on finding boundaries to push.

Between 1970 and 1975, Lennon released an album every year. He then spent five years on musical hiatus, focusing on his young son, Sean, and wife Yoko Ono. Lennon returned to the musical scene with *Double Fatasy*, an album alternating between songs performed by Lennon and by Ono. The album was falling after only three weeks on the U.K. charts, and

critics disdained it as a self-indulgent portrait of marriage that might or might not have reflected their domestic reality.

But Lennon wasn't particularly interested in critical acclaim, as he made clear in his 1980 *Rolling Stone* interview: "These critics, with the illusions they've created about artists — it's like idol worship. They only like people when they're on their way up ... I cannot be on the way up again. ... What they want is dead heroes, like Sid Vicious and James Dean. I'm not interesting in being a dead [expletive] hero. ... So forget 'em, forget 'em."

He may have had a point: When he was murdered, sales of *Double Fantasy* went through the roof and criticism was muted — in some cases, even withdrawn from publication.

Paul McCartney

It's impossible to sum up Paul McCartney's post-Beatles accomplishments in anything shorter than a book. After all, he has spent more than 40 years as an ex-Beatle. Along with fronting the band Wings, many solo outings and a couple of film projects, he also dipped his toe in the classical scene and collaborated anonymously on electronic music experiments.

"I never thought that I'd particularly be doing anything," he told NPR in 2000. "I'm not one of these people who has a vision or has a plan of what I'm doing. I'm just letting it unfold. What I'm lucky enough to be part of, and what leads me into something, I'm quite receptive to. Sometimes people would say too receptive 'cause I accept things like the Liverpool Oratorio … I was just asked … would I do anything for the Liverpool Orchestra? I said, 'Yeah! Sure!' without really realizing … how much work was involved."

Paul in 2013.

REX FEATURES VIA AP IMAGES

Paul's Highlight

It's difficult to pick a high point for a legendary career spanning four decades. Perhaps 1979, when the *Guinness Book of Records* declared Paul the most successful popular music composer ever, or 1997, when he was knighted for his musical contributions. But the ultimate tribute to Paul is where he is right now. At age 71, he has released *New*, his 16th studio album, to acclaim. The album is a blend of reminiscence and rebirth; one song focuses on his pre-Beatles days, another on his new wife, Nancy Shevell. One of the four producers who worked on the records was Giles Martin, the son of George Martin.

Pitchfork writes, "it's gratifying and inspiring to see the pop musician who arguably most deserves to rest on his laurels steadfastly refuse to do so. But even more remarkable than his work ethic is the fact that he's still trying to improve himself as an artist."

Paul's Lowlight

Even geniuses hit sour notes, and McCartney's came with *Press to Play* in 1986. Angling for a modern sound, he selected wunderkind producer Hugh Padgham, who had worked with The Police and Peter Gabriel, and he pulled in big-name guests like Eric Stewart and Pete Townshend. But work on the album dragged out for an agonizing 18 months, and everything went badly. Padgham and Stewart competed over producing duties and had even more trouble trying to tell McCartney the material was weak.

"It's difficult to tell Paul McCartney, isn't it?" Stewart said. "He's a great singer, he's written the greatest songs of all time, and you're saying, 'That's not good enough.'"

Padgham's memories were even less pleasant: "There was this conflict there. And that was something that Paul could do. He could actually wither you with a sentence if he didn't like what you said." When the album was finally released, the producers' worst fears were realized, and the effort marked McCartney's first studio collection ever to fall short of the U.S. top 20.

McCartney has suffered a lot of abuse for gravitating toward the schmaltzy ("My Love") and the silly ("Let 'Em In"). The criticism isn't entirely undeserved (if you've never seen Dana Carvey's sendups of McCartney specifically and of vapid pop music generally as Derek Stevens, check him out on YouTube). **McCartney seems to take it in stride, living well with his best revenge in "Silly Love Songs," a No. 1 hit in the U.S.**

AP PHOTO / J. GLANVILL

Paul and Linda McCartney harmonize during a Wings concert in 1976.

George with Ravi
Shankar in 1970.

George's Lowlight

"My Sweet Lord" was the biggest-selling single of 1971 in Britain. But it was also at the center of a high-profile plagiarism suit for its similarity to the 1963 Chiffons hit "He's So Fine." It became a sordid episode. The Beatles' business manager, Allen Klein, entered into negotiations with Bright Tunes, the owner of the track, to resolve the issue on Harrison's behalf by offering to buy the financially ailing publisher's entire catalog, but no settlement could be reached before the company was forced into receivership. While that was going on, Harrison, Lennon and Starr all cut ties with Klein in 1973, which led to more lawsuits. Harrison offered to settle with Bright Tunes but was rejected; as it turned out, Klein was still trying to purchase the company and was supplying it with financial details in Harrison's suit. The case reached district court in 1976, and Harrison was found to have "subconsciously" plagiarized the earlier tune, but the legal machinations and repercussions would continue for years afterward. Litigation between Klein and Harrison lasted into the 1990s.

George Harrison

Before the Beatles' breakup, Harrison had already recorded and released two solo albums and was probably the Beatle best positioned for a solo career. In 1970, he released the highly regarded album, *All Things Must Pass*, and the following year, he organized a charity event, the Concert for Bangladesh, that led to the release of a live triple album and, in 1972, a concert film. The event would go on to form the template for Live Aid, Farm Aid and pretty much every other musical charity event since.

Harrison continued to release new albums through the 1970s, but with waning commercial and critical success. In the early 1980s he stepped away almost entirely, taking a five-year break from recording. In 1987, he got back in the game, working with Jeff Lynne on a new album and collaborating with Ringo Starr, Eric Clapton and Elton John. The result was *Cloud Nine*, which included Harrison's rendition of James Ray's catchy, if repetitive "Got My Mind Set on You," which would be Harrison's biggest solo hit since "My Sweet Lord."

George's Highlight

Buoyed by the success of *Cloud Nine*, Harrison formed the Traveling Wilburys, a band of sorts that featured Harrison, Lynne, Bob Dylan, Tom Petty and Roy Orbison. "He just said he had a lot of fun with the Wilburys, and he had a lot of fun with the Beatles," Harrison's widow, Olivia, told Spinner.com in 2012. "I don't think there's anything you can compare to being in a band like the Beatles, is there? But he really had fun with Bob and Roy and Tom and Jeff. He loved being a collaborator and loved not having to do all the work himself. I think that was the main thing. And he could hang out; he liked to hang out. He didn't always have guys and musicians to hang out with. He missed that." The Wilburys released two albums, *Volume 1* in 1988 and *Volume 3* in 1990.

Humor fans owe a debt of **gratitude to Harrison for mortgaging his home to finance production of Monty Python's *Life of Brian*. Harrison founded the movie company HandMade Films to finance the film and went on to serve as executive producer for 23 more films with HandMade.** Here he poses with Madonna, the star of HandMade's *Shanghai Surprise*, released in 1986.

Ringo Starr

The least musically successful of the Beatles post-breakup, Starr has hardly been idle and can claim notable accomplishments in painting — he recently had an exhibit of works he made with the software MS Paint — film and music.

Despite being the oldest Beatle, he also has the most child-like reputation, so it's fitting that he was the original narrator for the preschooler show *Thomas the Tank Engine*, released an *Octopus Garden* children's book, and served as an honorary Santa Tracker and voice-over personality in 2003 and 2004 during the annual NORAD Tracks Santa program.

Starr is still recording and touring with various iterations of an All Starr Band, as he has done since 1989. "I am making records," he told CNN in 2012. "I am going on tour, and then I am off to do whatever else I want to do. So I have a very good life." O

Ringo became a children's book author in 2013.

PRESS ASSOCIATION VIA AP IMAGES

Ringo's Lowlight

As with his former bandmates, the early 1980s were unkind to Starr, starting with his 1981 album *Stop and Smell the Roses*. An interview with Merv Griffin hints at the chaos of the recording sessions: "It's interesting for me, when you don't have a band, you work with a lot of different musicians, and you work with guys who have bands. I just get on the kit to give the drummer a drink. I've been in three bands on this album and never seen the drummer." The album tanked, leading RCA to drop his contract. No major U.S. or U.K. label showed any interest in picking up his 1983 follow-up, *Old Wave*. RCA Canada finally released that album, which did poorly in all markets. It would be almost a decade before Starr would go back into the studio.

Ringo's Highlight

Musically, Starr peaked early. His most successful singles were "Photograph" from 1973 and "You're Sixteen" from 1974, both of which reached No. 1 in the United States. In 1972, he released his most successful U.K. single, "Back Off Boogaloo," which peaked at No. 2.

In 1981, Starr played the lead role in the hilariously bad movie *Caveman*. **"What we needed was a charming, romantic star who was short and unprepossessing,"** writer-director Carl Gottleib told an interviewer in 1981. "After Robin Williams, Dustin Hoffman and Dudley Moore, who is there? The casting chief Lynn Stallmaster suggested Ringo Starr, and I said, 'Right!'" The movie is so awful that it essentially ended Starr's career in movies, but it also is notable for another reasons: **Starr met and married Bond girl Barbara Bach during production.**

AP PHOTO / MBR / HERALD EXAMINER

The Beatles' U.S. Collection

The Beatles released 20 studio albums in North America between 1964 and 1970. The band also released several live albums and compilations.

Introducing the Beatles
January 1964

I Saw Her Standing There
Misery
Anna (Go To Him)
Chains
Boys
Love Me Do
PS I Love You
Baby It's You
Do You Want To Know A Secret
A Taste Of Honey
There's A Place
Twist And Shout

Meet The Beatles!
January 1964

I Want To Hold Your Hand
I Saw Her Standing There
This Boy
It Won't Be Long
All I've Got To Do
All My Loving
Don't Bother Me
Little Child
Till There Was You
Hold Me Tight
I Wanna Be Your Man
Not A Second Time

The Beatles' Second Album
April 1964

Roll Over Beethoven
Thank You Girl
You Really Got A Hold On Me
Devil In Her Heart
Money (That's What I Want)
You Can't Do That
Long Tall Sally
I Call Your Name
Please Mister Postman
I'll Get You
She Loves You

A Hard Day's Night
June 1964

A Hard Day's Night
Tell Me Why
I'll Cry Instead
I Should Have Known Better (instrumental)
I'm Happy Just To Dance With You
And I Love Her (instrumental)
I Should Have Known Better
If I Fell
And I Love Her
Ringo's Theme (This Boy) (instrumental)
Can't Buy Me Love
A Hard Day's Night (instrumental)

Something New
July 1964

I'll Cry Instead
Things We Said Today
Any Time At All
When I Get Home
Slow Down
Matchbox
Tell Me Why
And I Love Her
I'm Happy Just To Dance With You
If I Fell
Komm, Gib Mir Deine Hand

The Beatles' Story
November 1964

On Stage With The Beatles
How Beatlemania Began
Beatlemania In Action
Man Behind The Beatles - Brian Epstein
John Lennon
Who's A Millionaire?
Beatles Will Be Beatles
Man Behind The Music — George Martin
George Harrison
A Hard Day's Night — Their First Movie
Paul McCartney
Sneaky Haircuts And More About Paul
The Beatles Look At Life
"Victims" Of Beatlemania
Beatle Medley
Ringo Starr
Liverpool And All the World!

Beatles '65
December 1964

No Reply
I'm A Loser
Baby's In Black
Rock And Roll Music
I'll Follow The Sun
Mr Moonlight
Honey Don't
I'll Be Back
She's A Woman
I Feel Fine
Everybody's Trying To Be My Baby

The Early Beatles
March 1965

Love Me Do
Twist And Shout
Anna (Go To Him)
Chains
Boys
Ask Me Why
Please Please Me
PS I Love You
Baby It's You
A Taste Of Honey
Do You Want To Know A Secret

Beatles VI
June 1965

Kansas City/Hey-Hey-Hey-Hey!
Eight Days A Week
You Like Me Too Much
Bad Boy
I Don't Want To Spoil The Party
Words Of Love
What You're Doing
Yes It Is
Dizzy Miss Lizzy
Tell Me What You See
Every Little Thing

Help!
August 1965

Help!
The Night Before
From Me To You Fantasy (instrumental)
You've Got To Hide Your Love Away
I Need You
In The Tyrol (instrumental)
Another Girl
Another Hard Day's Night (instrumental)
Ticket To Ride
The Bitter End/You Can't Do That
(instrumental)
You're Going To Lose That Girl
The Chase (instrumental)

The Beatles' U.S. Collection

Rubber Soul
December 1965

I've Just Seen A Face
Norwegian Wood (This Bird Has Flown)
You Won't See Me
Think For Yourself
The Word
Michelle
It's Only Love
Girl
I'm Looking Through You
In My Life
Wait
Run For Your Life
Twist And Shout

Yesterday... And Today
June 1966

Drive My Car
I'm Only Sleeping
Nowhere Man
Doctor Robert
Yesterday
Act Naturally
And Your Bird Can Sing
If I Needed Someone
We Can Work It Out
What Goes On
Day Tripper

Revolver
August 1966

Taxman
Eleanor Rigby
Love You To
Here, There And Everywhere
Yellow Submarine
She Said She Said
Good Day Sunshine
For No One
I Want To Tell You
Got To Get You Into My Life
Tomorrow Never Knows

Sgt. Pepper's Lonely Hearts Club Band
June 1967

Sgt Pepper's Lonely Hearts Club Band
With A Little Help From My Friends
Lucy In The Sky With Diamonds
Getting Better
Fixing A Hole
She's Leaving Home
Being For The Benefit Of Mr Kite!
Within You Without You
When I'm Sixty-Four
Lovely Rita
Good Morning Good Morning
Sgt Pepper's Lonely Hearts Club Band (Reprise)
A Day In The Life

Magical Mystery Tour
November 1967

Magical Mystery Tour
The Fool On The Hill
Flying
Blue Jay Way
Your Mother Should Know
I Am The Walrus
Hello, Goodbye
Strawberry Fields Forever
Penny Lane
Baby You're A Rich Man
All You Need Is Love

The Beatles (White Album)
November 1968

Back In The USSR
Dear Prudence
Glass Onion
Ob-La-Di, Ob-La-Da
Wild Honey Pie
The Continuing Story Of Bungalow Bill
While My Guitar Gently Weeps
Happiness Is A Warm Gun
Martha My Dear
I'm So Tired
Blackbird
Piggies
Rocky Raccoon
Don't Pass Me By
Why Don't We Do It In The Road?
I Will
Julia
Birthday
Yer Blues
Mother Nature's Son
Everybody's Got Something To Hide (Except Me And My Monkey)
Sexy Sadie
Helter Skelter
Long, Long, Long
Revolution 1
Honey Pie
Savoy Truffle
Cry Baby Cry
Revolution 9
Good Night

Yellow Submarine
January 1969

Yellow Submarine
Only A Northern Song
All Together Now
Hey Bulldog
It's All Too Much
All You Need Is Love
Pepperland
Sea Of Time
Sea Of Holes
Sea Of Monsters
March Of The Meanies
Pepperland Laid Waste
Yellow Submarine In Pepperland

Abbey Road
October 1969

Come Together
Something
Maxwell's Silver Hammer
Oh! Darling
Octopus's Garden
I Want You (She's So Heavy)
Here Comes The Sun
Because
You Never Give Me Your Money
Sun King
Mean Mr Mustard
Polythene Pam
She Came In Through The Bathroom Window
Golden Slumbers
Carry That Weight
The End
Her Majesty

Hey Jude
February 1970

Can't Buy Me Love
I Should Have Known Better
Paperback Writer
Rain
Lady Madonna
Revolution
Hey Jude
Old Brown Shoe
Don't Let Me Down
The Ballad Of John And Yoko

Let It Be
May 1970

Two Of Us
Dig A Pony
Across The Universe
I Me Mine
Dig It
Let It Be
Maggie Mae
I've Got A Feeling
One After 909
The Long And Winding Road
For You Blue
Get Back

5 Fifth Beatles

The Fab Four had more than a little help from their friends along the way.

BY
ARWEN
BICKNELL

George Harrison observed at one point that "there are supposed to have been 5,000 Fifth Beatles." That may be a conservative estimate.

There may be no more coveted title in the world of music, or one that's been more widely handed out by journalists and fans. Candidates range across time and place — from the band's earliest influences to its inner circle of longtime confidants, from ex-girlfriends to widows, from solitary DJs in the U.S. to the entire town of Liverpool. It's an honorific equally revered and ubiquitous.

Here are the top contenders for the title.

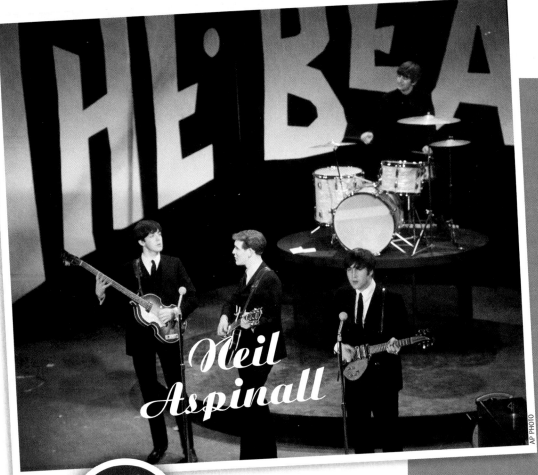

"Maybe Neil Aspinall said 'No' too many times, but his overriding thought was always to protect the four Beatles in the frenzy that he had to deal with. No one can imagine the stress of handling the group, for everyone in the world wanted them. His business decisions were sound, and the fact that the Beatles are acknowledged to be the greatest of our stars is his legacy."
— *George Martin*

5 Neil Aspinall

Neil Aspinall was a childhood friend of Paul McCartney and George Harrison. He became the Beatles' road manager and personal assistant, and then later the manager of Apple Corps.

In Beatles' lore, Aspinall is known for the affair he had with Pete Best's mother, Mona. They had a son in July 1962; a month later, Pete Best was cut from the band. Aspinall worked closely with manager Brian Epstein, stood in for an ill George Harrison during rehearsals for the *Ed Sullivan Show* (pictured above), and signed sets of Beatles' autographs for thousands of unsuspecting fans. He was charged with sourcing photographs for all the people shown on the *Sgt. Pepper's* cover and was asked to manage Apple Corps, founded in April 1968. In the early 1990s he was appointed executive producer of *The Beatles Anthology* project, which had its roots in the 1970s as a film called *The Long And Winding Road*. Producer George Martin once said Aspinall was the true Fifth Beatle.

"Neil was a great man who I knew even before I met any of the guys in the Beatles. I met him at school when we were both 11 and we remained friends ever since."
— *Paul McCartney*

From a 1996 interview with Aspinall in MOJO:

Q: Even George Martin describes you as the Fifth Beatle. How do you feel about that?

A: Oh, I keep trying to lay that on George! There is no Fifth Beatle. I think if there was such a thing, it would be Pete Best or Stu Sutcliffe, not some outsider who wasn't in the band. A ridiculous suggestion.

"There are supposed to be about 5,000 Fifth Beatles. But really there were only two: Derek Taylor and Neil Aspinall."
— *George Harrison*

Pete Best

Technically, the argument could be made that Ringo Starr became the Fifth Beatle (maybe the sixth, if you count Stuart Sutcliffe) upon replacing Pete Best as drummer. Best met the band because his mother, Mona, owned the Casbah, where they performed, and he joined the group at the invitation of Paul McCartney in 1960, a day before the Beatles' first trip to Hamburg.

Best's quiet personality and aloofness from the rest of the group meant he tended not to participate in their banter, and he was the only member not to get what would later be known as a Beatle haircut. When the band auditioned for George Martin in 1962, Martin felt Best's drumming was substandard, and the group cut him. There was speculation later that his standoffish attitude was also a factor, or even that he was cut from the band because the other members were jealous of the attention he received from female fans.

"It was a big issue at the time, how we dumped Pete. And I do feel sorry for him, because of what he could have been on to, but as far as we were concerned, it was strictly a professional decision. If he wasn't up to the mark — slightly in our eyes, and definitely in the producer's eyes — then there was no choice. But it was still very difficult. It is one of the most difficult things we ever had to do."
— *Paul McCartney*

"Some people expect me to be bitter and twisted, but I'm not. I feel very fortunate in my life. God knows what strains and stresses the Beatles must have been under. They became a public commodity. John paid for that with his life."
— *Pete Best*

4

"We were cowards. We got Epstein to do the dirty work for us."
— *John Lennon*

Pete Best

AP PHOTO

3

Stuart Sutcliffe

Stuart Sutcliffe was an artist and the band's original bassist in Liverpool and Hamburg. In addition to performing with the group, he also arranged bookings for them and occasionally allowed them to rehearse in his flat.

Despite Lennon's claim that the Beatles' name came in a dream when a man on a flaming pie gave him the idea, it was actually Lennon and Sutcliffe's combined idea to change the band's name from The Quarrymen. The name Beatles was a pun inspired by Buddy Holly's group, The Crickets, and it went through a number of variations: the Silver Beatles, Silver Beats, Silver Beetles, and Silver Beatles once more before settling in as just the Beatles in August 1960.

In July 1961, Sutcliffe decided to leave the group to focus on painting (some of his artwork is pictured here). The band attempted to add a new bass player before handing over bass duties to McCartney, who had previously played piano and guitar. Sutcliffe died of a cerebral hemorrhage in 1962 at the age of 21.

"I looked up to Stu. I depended on him to tell me the truth. Stu would tell me if something was good and I'd believe him."

— John Lennon

"The Beatles were best when Stuart was still in the band. To me it had more balls, it was even more rock 'n' roll when Stuart was playing the bass and Paul was playing piano or another guitar. The band was, somehow, as a rock 'n' roll band, more complete."
— Klaus Voorman, who played bass with the band during the early days

"Stu had won a painting competition. The prize was 75 quid (about $150). We said to him, 'That's exactly the price of a Hofner bass!' He said, 'It's supposed to be for painting materials,' but we managed to persuade him."
— Paul McCartney

Brian Epstein

②

Brian Epstein

From the Beatles' first success until his death of a drug overdose in August 1967, Brian Epstein took care of every aspect of the Beatles' career. He discovered the Beatles and guided the band to stardom. He cleaned up their image, coaxing them from blue jeans and leather jackets to matching suits. He even paid for them to record a demo with Decca.

After the band had been rejected by nearly all the major recording studios in London, he secured their contract with producer George Martin at EMI and took on the unpleasant task of firing Pete Best as drummer. He was an ardent supporter of their writing in a time when a group writing all of their music and lyrics themselves was nearly unheard of, and he took the concept of rock promotion to new limits with stadium concerts and world tours.

On a personal basis, Epstein suffered the same sort of abuse and insults from the band as many other members of the inner circle; in his case, being Jewish and gay made him an easy target. Upon his death, things slowly unraveled until the group's dissolution three years later.

"Brian Epstein had a big posh car. Early on it was great because Paul and I had learnt how to drive and we always wanted to drive his car. That's one of the reasons we signed up with him — because he had a good car." — *George Harrison*

"If anyone was the Fifth Beatle, it was Brian. People talked about George Martin as being the Fifth Beatle because of his musical involvement but, particularly in the early days, Brian was very much part of the group."
— *Paul McCartney*

The Fifth Beetle?

The Beatles strolling across the street on the album cover of *Abbey Road* is one of the most iconic images in music history. It has inspired countless imitations and spawned a mass of conspiracy theories. Some of these theories centered around the so-called fifth Beetle — a white Volkswagen Beetle on the left-hand side of the image. The car's license plate reads LMW 28IF; 28 was the age conspiracy theorists said Paul would have been if he hadn't "died." It was also said that LMW stands for "Linda McCartney Weeps." On a more mundane note, the owners reported their license plate being stolen countless times after the album's release.

"After Brian died, we collapsed. Paul took over and supposedly led us. But what is leading us, when we went round in circles? We broke up then. That was the disintegration."
— *John Lennon*

AP PHOTO / PA

George Martin

1

George Martin

If there is any one person who deserves to be called the Fifth Beatle, it's George Martin. Except for some post-production work by Phil Spector on *Let It Be*, Martin produced every Beatles recording from start to finish. He gave the group its first recording contract and his talent as a producer and arranger made him a key contributor to the group's sound in the studio.

Martin wrote many orchestral arrangements with the band. His effect can be identified in the string quartet on "Yesterday" and the symphony work on "A Day in the Life." He performed the harpsichord solo on "In My Life," while "Being for the Benefit of Mr. Kite!" showcases his work on the organ. He oversaw post-production on 1995's *The Beatles Anthology* (pictured above with Ringo, Paul and George), although he

> ## "George was the only person who took a chance on us to make a record. Every other label turned us down."
> — *Ringo Starr*

> "If Paul wanted to use violins, [Martin] would translate it for him. Like 'In My Life,' there is an Elizabethan piano solo in it, so he would do things like that. We would say, 'Play like Bach,' or something, so he would put 12 bars in there. He helped us develop a language, to talk to musicians."
> — *John Lennon*

> "George Martin [was] quite experimental for who he was, a grown-up."
> — *Paul McCartney*

turned over production of the two new singles ("Free as a Bird" and "Real Love") to Jeff Lynne.

With all that, it was often a thankless job. He met with resistance from McCartney on many arranging ideas, and Lennon was positively vicious toward him in letters and interviews around the time of the band's breakup. ◐

Arwen Bicknell works as an editor at the RAND Corporation, and lives in Virginia. At her wedding, she walked down the aisle to "In My Life," which is her favorite Beatles' song.

Honorable Mentions

Derek Taylor: The band's publicist and a member of its inner circle, Taylor started working for the group in 1963 and worked with the band and Apple Corps for over 30 years.

Mal Evans: The Beatles' road manager and personal assistant, Evans joined the band in 1963 as a security guard. He and Neil Aspinall collaborated closely to protect the Beatles' privacy and cope with public demand.

Astrid Kirchherr/Klaus Voormann/Jurgen Vollmer: This trio connected with the band during the Beatles' Hamburg days. Voormann played bass for a handful of Hamburg gigs after Stuart Sutcliffe quit the band, and he also designed the album cover for *Revolver*, which netted him a Grammy. Vollmer and Kirchherr, both artists, shared credit for overhauling the Beatles' style, including their haircuts, and are noted for their photos of the band taken at this time. Sutcliffe and Kirchherr were engaged when Sutcliffe died.

Billy Preston: Keyboardist Preston played on the *Let It Be* and *Abbey Road* albums. His contribution was acknowledged when the Beatles issued "Get Back" as "The Beatles with Billy Preston." Preston also performed with Lennon, Harrison and Starr after the Beatles broke up.

Murray the K: Disc jockey Murray Kaufman reached his peak of popularity in the mid-1960s when, as the top-rated radio host in New York, he became an early and ardent supporter and friend of the band. He gave himself the moniker of the "Fifth Beatle," and Ringo and Paul laughingly endorsed his claim to the title in *Anthology* interviews. He was the first DJ the Beatles welcomed into their circle, and they often called his show to give exclusive interviews.

Jeff Lynne: Electric Light Orchestra frontman Lynne worked with McCartney, Harrison, and Starr on solo projects, becoming especially close with Harrison, who invited him to join the Traveling Wilburys. Lynne produced the two reunion singles that resulted from *The Beatles Anthology* project ("Free as a Bird" and "Real Love").

Eric Clapton: Clapton performed lead guitar on "While My Guitar Gently Weeps" and is one of the few musicians who appeared on solo recordings by each of the four Beatles after the band broke up.

Yoko Ono: Often blamed for the band's breakup, Ono was a presence in the recording studio after 1968. Her voice can be heard on "The Continuing Story of Bungalow Bill," "Birthday" and "Revolution 9." She had a strong voice in Beatles-related decisions when Lennon was alive, and since his death, she has wielded enormous influence over the band's legacy.

Andy White/Jimmie Nicol: White was the professional drummer hired for "Love Me Do" when producer George Martin was unhappy with the work of both Pete Best and Ringo Starr. When Starr became ill during the band's 1964 tour, Nicol filled in as drummer for the Dutch and Danish legs of the tour.

Little Richard: An early influence for the band, Little Richard has occasionally claimed the Fifth Beatle title for his own. At the Beatles' induction to the Rock and Roll Hall of Fame, Harrison backed him up: "It's all his fault, really."

The Man Who Hit Pause

Throughout 1963, the fate of the Beatles rested in the hands of one man: Dave Dexter.

BY
KENNETH
WOMACK

n 1975, the Beatles' first manager, Allan Williams, titled his autobiography *The Man Who Gave the Beatles Away*. In so doing, he recognized his own complicity in failing to capitalize on the band's budding musical genius — a role that fell in November 1961 to Brian Epstein, the band's second manager and the eventual architect of Beatlemania.

In 1962 and 1963, despite the Beatles' popularity in the U.K., they were ignored in the United States. Capitol Records' Dave Dexter (left) repeatedly rejected the Fab Four's records until he was forced to release "I Want to Hold Your Hand" in December 1963.

Williams was only the first in a long line of gatekeepers who failed to recognize the Beatles' greatness. Take Dick Rowe, for example. As the head A&R man for Decca Records, Rowe notoriously passed on signing the Beatles after their January 1962 audition, infamously remarking that "groups with guitars are on the way out."

In terms of neglecting to appreciate the group's early potential, Williams and Rowe are rivaled only by Dave E. Dexter Jr., the longtime Capitol Records employee who steadfastly refused to release the Beatles' runaway British hits stateside. When American Beatlemania reached its apex, Dexter was instrumental in repackaging the Beatles for the American marketplace, cannibalizing their original U.K. releases and adding echo and reverb to alter their sound.

A Great Jazz Man

Born in Kansas City, Mo., in 1915, Dexter began his career as a music journalist in the 1930s and 1940s with the *Kansas City Journal Post* and later with *Down Beat* magazine. A jazz aficionado with a well-honed ear, Dexter produced an album titled *Kansas City Jazz* that traced the history of the Kansas City jazz scene through the work of such artists as Count Basie and Big Joe Turner.

In 1943, Dexter joined fledgling Capitol Records as a publicity officer, eventually becoming the company's influential international A&R representative. During this period, he attracted a number of celebrated artists to Capitol, including Frank Sinatra, Peggy Lee, Stan Kenton, Nat King Cole, Duke Ellington and Woody Herman. Dexter also achieved considerable renown for his efforts producing the Duke Ellington jazz standard "Satin Doll."

In 1944, Dexter produced *The History of Jazz*, a series of four albums. According to jazz historian Floyd Levin, Dexter "conceived the idea, assembled the impressive array of musicians and personally supervised the entire project. To this day, those great recordings remain among the most ambitious anthologies of jazz history."

Dexter was a legitimate jazz guru — he understood the music, both how to create it and how to package it. But by the 1950s, Dexter was deriding changes in popular music, particularly the rise of rock 'n' roll artists such as Elvis Presley, whom he described as "juvenile and maddeningly repetitive."

"The Worst Thing I'd Ever Heard"

In the early 1960s, Dexter's influence at Capitol Records had become so significant that company president Alan W. Livingston authored a June 1962 memo in which he instructed his colleagues to submit all albums from outside the U.S. to Dexter for his consideration and approval.

Capitol could choose to release albums in the U.S. that had been released internationally by Capitol's parent company, the EMI Group. EMI was the Beatles' record company in Britain. That meant it fell to Dave Dexter to decide whether the Beatles would make it in America.

In October 1962, Dexter opted not to release the Beatles' "Love Me Do" single. He followed suit in early 1963 and rejected "Please Please Me" and "From Me to You," which were subsequently released by Vee-Jay Records. Soon thereafter, Dexter passed on the option to release "She Loves You," which had emerged as the U.K.'s best-selling single of all time at that juncture.

Differing Discographies

These examples illustrate how different Beatles albums were in the U.S. and U.K.

■ The Beatles' second album in the U.K. was *With the Beatles*. Released in November 1963, its 14 songs include "All My Loving," "Roll Over Beethoven" and "Money." Nine of the 14 songs were included in the U.S. release *Meet the Beatles*, Capitol's first Beatles album. *Meet the Beatles* also included one track from the Beatles' first U.K. album and two B-sides.

■ The U.S. release *The Beatles' Second Album* used the rest of the five songs from the U.K.'s *With the Beatles* but also picked up Beatles songs from singles and two other U.K. albums.

■ *Help!* was released in August 1965 in both the U.S. and U.K. In the U.S. it included seven Beatles' songs and padded out with orchestral arrangements from the movie. In the U.K. it had 14 Beatles' songs and no orchestral arrangements.

■ The masterpiece *Revolver* contained 14 songs in its U.K. version. In the U.S. three of these songs — "I'm Only Sleeping," "And Your Bird Can Sing" and "Doctor Robert" — were simply lopped off because they had been included in an earlier U.S. release.

■ It wasn't until *Sgt. Pepper's* in 1967 that U.S. fans would experience an album the way the Beatles had intended it to be heard.

Dave Dexter was a jazz man and worked with some of the best jazz musicians and bandleaders of the 1940s and 1950s, including Benny Goodman, the "King of Swing" (below) and the incomparable Count Basie (center with Dexter and Glenn Wallichs, one of the founders of Capitol Records).

"She Loves You" was subsequently optioned by Philadelphia's Swan Records. Vee-Jay and Swan were small companies that lacked promotional muscle. Those early stateside efforts by the Beatles went largely unnoticed.

In a 1988 interview, Dexter recalled the first time that he heard "Please Please Me:" "The British companies — they wanted us to issue as many of their records over here as possible because [the U.S.] was the biggest record market in the world. And I can only remember when I heard Lennon playing the harmonica on this record, I thought it was the worst thing I'd ever heard."

EMI racked up nearly 300,000 advance orders in Britain for *With the Beatles* in the fall of 1963. EMI could no longer wait for its American subsidiary — meaning Dexter — to come around. Capitol was ordered by EMI's managing director, L.G. Wood, to release the Beatles' next single without delay. Having originally planned to press a mere 5,000 copies of "I Want to Hold Your Hand," Capitol earmarked the impressive $50,000 to promote the single in the United States. The Beatles appeared on the *Ed Sullivan Show*, and American Beatlemania was born.

Things We Said Today

In a memo he sent Feb. 20, 1964, Dexter defended himself to Livingston, writing that "Alan, I make errors in judgment as does everyone else, but when you consider the enormous amount of singles and albums sent to my desk every month … I am frankly amazed that we do not miss out on more hits as the months and years go by."

Subsequently asked by Livingston to write a detailed report about the records that he had passed on during the previous year, specifically the Beatles, Dexter wrote in an Oct. 1, 1964, memo: "In a carton containing 17 other singles, I received 'Love Me Do' and 'P.S. I Love You'; [I] was not impressed, and so informed Tony Palmer [Dexter's EMI counterpart] by checking a 6x4 form and airmailing it back to him that same day."

As he notes in the memo, Dexter changed his tune in late summer, writing that "by the time I returned from England in August of 1963, it was apparent that the Beatles were the hottest thing England had ever encountered, and when I learned that Swan had waived on the group, I then somewhat hysterically started urging Livingston, Gilmore and Dunn to exert every possible pressure on EMI and Epstein."

Dexter's efforts to defend himself paid off. Despite failing repeatedly to see the band's commercial possibilities, Dexter was now responsible for overseeing their U.S. promotion. In this role, he remixed their songs, adding reverb and echo, thinking that his tinkering would give the music more of a "live" feel and make it more palatable for the American audience.

In so doing, Dexter affected considerable sonic changes on Beatles' records for their American release, a process that many Beatles fans and historians refer to as "Dexterization." Although there are fans of the Dexter versions — and Dexter's tinkering clearly did not stand in the way of the Beatles' success — overall, they lack the balance, warmth and sense of clarity that the band's U.K. releases enjoyed.

For rock critic Dave Marsh, "The real question is: How did Dave Dexter retain such control over the fate of the Beatles' American record releases? His tenure, from 1963 to 1966, covers by far the most important part of the Beatles' career. He not only delayed their appearance on a major label in this country for more than a year, he then proceeded to fiddle with every product that the Beatles sent to the States, not only making weird and inexcusable judgments about song choices and sequences but also doing a very bad job of getting the music he was sent mixed and mastered for final release."

In addition to manipulating the Beatles' sound, Dexter rejected both the cover art and the track listings for the band's original U.K. album releases, opting instead to revamp them for stateside consumption. In many ways, Dexter's decisions to alter the Beatles' cover artwork was a matter of subjective taste.

As Dexter wrote in a Sept. 2, 1965, memo to Livingston: "We consider our artwork in virtually every case superior to the English front cover art, artistically as well as commercially. Ours is slanted more to the merchandising end; we also use more color than EMI." In that same memo, Dexter defended his effort to reduce the number of tracks on the band's American releases, writing that "no Capitol LP is ever identical in repertoire to the British LP ... Because EMI persists in the 14-track package, we will never be in position to release them simultaneously."

After the release of *Revolver* in 1966, Dexter was no longer in a position to manipulate the Beatles' sound, although the damage had already been done. American fans would be subject almost exclusively to Dexterized versions of the band's pre-1967 releases until the release of the Beatles on CD in 1987. The Dexter versions are now available in two boxed sets, *The Capitol Albums*, *Volume 1* and *Volume 2*, but have otherwise been replaced by the music the Beatles intended to release.

Later Years

By 1966, Dexter had been demoted from his influential post as A&R representative. In the 1970s, Dexter left Capitol altogether, eventually landing an editorial position with *Billboard* magazine. Following Lennon's assassination on Dec. 8, 1980, Dexter became a flashpoint for Beatles fans yet again, writing a notorious article in *Billboard* in which he criticized the recently fallen Beatle. Dexter's article, published 12 days after Lennon's murder, was titled "Nobody's Perfect: Lennon's Ego and Intransigence Irritated Those Who Knew Him."

In his diatribe, Dexter wrote that "no pop artist since the early 1960s was more musically gifted than John Lennon. And of the four Beatles, Lennon was — among those in the industry who worked with him — the most disliked." Remarkably, Dexter goes on to recount Lennon and the Beatles' various failures, including the fact that they broke up when there was a financial bonanza to be had by staying together.

Dexter concluded that "Lennon will be remembered well for his musical contributions. Unlike himself, there was nothing eccentric or unlikable about John's artistry. And that's what all of us will remember." Not surprisingly, Dexter's tasteless article raised the ire of *Billboard's* sponsors, forcing the magazine to publish a hasty apology.

In subsequent years, Dexter rounded out his career with additional music journalism and production efforts, while never really shaking his reputation as the man who got in the Beatles' way. Dexter passed away from complications from a stroke in April 1990 when he was 74.

As important as his contributions to American jazz truly were, Dexter will always be remembered as the record executive who passed, time and time again, on the early opportunity to release the Beatles' music stateside. As history has so resoundingly shown, he should've known better. ◉

Kenneth Womack teaches English and Integrative Arts at Penn State Altoona. He is the author or editor of four books devoted to the Beatles, including the forthcoming Beatles Encyclopedia: Everything Fab Four. *His favorite Beatles' song is "Happiness Is a Warm Gun."*

AP PHOTO

From ↻ Weak to
WOW

Prior to the Beatles, Capitol Records had a dismal track record releasing U.K. singles in the United States. Here are the numbers from 1961 to 1963, according to a memo Dave Dexter

1961

ARTIST	SALES
Michael Hill	1,418
Nelson Keene	65
Cliff Bennett	156
eter Sellers and Sophia Loren	186
Alma Cogan	154
Helen Shapiro release no. 1:	3,365
Helen Shapiro release no. 2:	101
Helen Shapiro release no. 3:	18,919

1962

ARTIST	SALES
Ricky Stevens	125
Helen Shapiro	4,149
Johnny De Little	403
Freddy Gardner	3,693
Mrs. Mills	72

1963

ARTIST	SALES
Grazina	446
Dick Kallman	1,370
Johnny Kid	96
Freddie & the Dreamers	105
Frank Ifield release no. 1:	54,716
Frank Ifield release no. 2:	71,666
THE BEATLES	**2,967,422**

Here Come The Sons

The Beatles have inspired many musicians — including their sons.

BY
MIKE
SHELLANS

All of the Beatles have sons who have pursued music professionally. Perhaps that's not so weird. But now consider this: All of the Beatles' sons have pursued musical careers.

For these men, being the son of a Beatle has been a double-edged sword. They attract attention and listeners just for being who they are. But the inevitable comparisons to their fathers raise the question: How can anyone stack up to a Beatle?

Julian Lennon

Julian Lennon was tied to pop music and the Beatles even as a child, having inspired John to compose "Lucy in the Sky with Diamonds" when he presented his dad with a drawing of a school friend. Paul McCartney composed "Hey Jude" (originally titled "Hey Jules") out of empathy for Julian during his parents' divorce.

Julian explored guitar, piano and drums growing up, playing drums on John's song "Ya Ya" from his *Walls and Bridges* album. He turned really serious about music after his father's death. Julian has released six albums to date: *Valotte* (1984), *The Secret Value of Daydreaming* (1986), *Mr. Jordan* (1989), *Help Yourself* (1991), *Photograph Smile* (1998) and *Everything Changes* (2011).

Download

"Saltwater" off the 1991 album *Help Yourself*. The strings and keyboard are reminiscent of "Strawberry Fields Forever" and the chords seem fresh yet familiar as Julian sings harmony with himself during the wonderfully contrasting bridge section. Steve Hunter's Beatles-style guitar solo brings together Julian's original ideas with riffs George Harrison sent to Julian when he was unable to make the recording session.

John with Julian

Julian Lennon

Julian looks like his father, and his sound and style do closely resemble John's, but his song writing reflects his own personality and perspective. He is a true talent. Julian's debut single, "Valotte," for example, released when he was just 21 years old, is a well-crafted, original pop song that showed Julian's emerging singing and piano skills. "Too Late for Goodbyes" has an engaging up-tempo reggae groove. Nods to John abound — the lyrics, vocal tricks such as bending the high notes, and the strong harmonica playing all bring to mind the senior Lennon. "Stick Around," from Julian's second album, offers us a maturing Julian, with richer lower register vocals than John and a 1980s synth-pop beat with a hard edge.

Julian has a gift for harmonizing, and this adds just the right musical icing to his songs. On his strong *Mr. Jordan* album, Julian teams up with guitarist John McCurry, an ironic progression from Lennon and McCartney in the '60s to Lennon and McCurry in the '80s. "Now You're in Heaven" is one of several standout pieces from Mr. Jordan, with Julian exploring both ends of his singing range over a heavy drum beat, synthesizers and exciting electric guitars.

Julian's Help Yourself album brought us the gorgeous "Saltwater," while "Day After Day" from *Photograph Smile* is a Beatles-esque love song complete with acoustic piano, string orchestra and George Harrison-style slide electric guitar.

Sean Lennon

Sean Lennon was born on John's 35th birthday, Oct. 9, 1975, and is the only child of John Lennon and Yoko Ono. John said of Sean: "He didn't come out of my belly but, by God, I made his bones, because I've attended to every meal, and to how he sleeps, and to the fact that he swims like a fish."

Sean was a celebrity from birth, and he took up bass and sang at an early age. He first sang on Yoko's 1984 album *Every Man Has a Woman*. Unlike his half-brother Julian, Sean delved into the more experimental side of pop music, signing with Adam Yauch of the Beastie Boys at the age of 23 and releasing *Into the Sun* in 1998.

One writer says of the album, "It has unexpectedly eclectic roots and a laid-back vibe." But songs such as "Queue" sound somewhat amateurish and undeveloped, borrowing at times from the Beach Boys and placing Sean's much-thinner-than-John's voice over inexpensive sounding synthesizers and off-the-cuff harmonies.

John with Sean

Sean Lennon

SHUTTERSTOCK / LOUIS BURGIS / KINGKONGPHOTO

EXPRESS NEWSPAPER/ VIA AP IMAGES

Download

"Dead Meat" from the 2006 album *Friendly Fire*. This track has a "You've Got to Hide Your Love Away" feel, with Sean's voice supported by acoustic guitars and strings. Lush harmonies and a gorgeous chord progression elevate the bridge section, and the string interlude takes us back to the Beatles' songs under George Martin. Sean's solid work on the rhythm guitar and purposeful vocals make this a top-notch cut.

After touring as guest bassist with Cibo Matto, an electronic pop rock duo from Japan, Sean released *Half Horse Half Musician* in 1999. "Heart and Lung" from that album showed Sean's voice maturing, but he tries too hard to project. The song has cute elements, with a synth clarinet melody, bells and percussion over '50s-style strummed acoustic guitars, but the best part occurs near the end, when Sean sings nonsense words very reminiscent of John's vocal ad-libs. His next album, *Friendly Fire*, didn't appear until 2006, and according to Allmusic.com, "As it stands, Sean's career is starting to seem like a rich kid's holiday, and *Friendly Fire* has the same feel as *Into the Sun*: namely, it's a pleasant but forgettable arty pop record made by a guy who has some promise but little discipline."

The title track for *Friendly Fire*, with its lovely strummed acoustic guitars and melodic electric bass, is a high point. The song is well-constructed, but even here it is clear that Sean simply wasn't born with a great natural singing voice, and his intonation can wander at times. He does stretch his range a bit at the song's end, with his voice's reedy quality working better at the upper end of his register.

In 2009, Sean composed the score for the film *Rosencrantz & Guildenstern Are Undead*, and bits such as "Elsinore Reprise" are delightful and right in his musical wheelhouse.

Zak Starkey

It seems only natural that Zak would take up drums, with father Ringo Starr (whose real name is Richard Starkey) holding down that chair with the Beatles. But Ringo said early on, "I won't let Zak be a drummer!"

When Zak was 9, Ringo said, "We've got a piano at home and he bashes it, I show him a chord. I think he will be a musician, in fact."

But Zak seemed destined to sit behind the kit. After one drum lesson from his dad, Zak taught himself, bashing away to records. Zak was performing by age 12, joining the garage band The Next as a teen and leaving home to work with the Spencer Davis group. The Who bassist John Entwistle produced Zak's next band, Nightfly, and Zak's '80s project with Eddie Har-

AP PHOTO

Download
"Overture" from 1998's *Who's Serious* album. Zak is the unmistakable center of musical attention in this cut from an album showcasing The Who working with the London Philharmonic Orchestra. Zak's energetic, driving beat gives the track life, and his precision is offset by a bit of wild abandon perhaps inherited from mentor Keith Moon. Listen as Zak makes every fill, kick and tempo change seamless and decidedly musical.

AP PHOTO / PAUL SPINELLI

Ringo and Maureen with their first baby, Zak. In 2010, The Who, including Zak Starkey on drums, performed at the Super Bowl in Florida.

Jason Starkey

Ringo's second son, Jason Starkey, once exclaimed, "Being Ringo Starr's son is the biggest drag of my life. It's a total pain." Yet Jason has explored music like his brother and father, playing drums and working as a road manager for such bands as Buddy Curtis and the Grasshoppers, the People's Friends, and with his brother in Musty Jack Sponge & The Exploding Nudists. Unfortunately, Jason's arrest for theft and problems with drugs have slowed his career, but he continues to drum with various groups.

din, *Wind in the Willows*, was a joint venture featuring Donovan, Jon Lord, Denny Laine and Billy Ocean.

By the mid 1980s, Zak had played with Roger Daltry and John Entwistle, and he shared the stage for a 1987 Aids Day benefit concert with rock luminaries Elton John, George Michael and Boy George, as well as jazz giant Herbie Hancock. In 1987, the band Musty Jack Sponge & The Exploding Nudists featured brothers Zak on guitar and Jason on drums. Zak spent the 1990s playing with artists like Joe Walsh in Ringo's All-Starr touring band.

After drumming for the short-lived band Face, Zak joined forces with The Who, starting with 1996's Quadrophenia Tour. Zak's first drum set was a gift from The Who's Keith Moon. No one could predict at that time that Ringo's son would eventually be Moon's replacement.

The Who guitarist Pete Townshend has said, "We're really pleased to have him in the band. He's just stunning. He's very easy to play with. Mind you, I'm very spoiled with drummers. Zak has a lot of karmic Keith Moon about him, which is wonderful. It's easy to make too much of that — he really is his own drummer. He has his own style. But he's very intelligent. What he did was adapt his own style as an imitator of Keith Moon, but he's modified that, moderated it, in a very intelligent and musical way so that he won't be directly compared."

Zak spent time drumming for the band Oasis, a Beatles-influenced band, in the early and mid-part of the millennium, but his commitments with The Who, including their spectacular half-time show at the 2010 Super Bowl, continue to keep him busy.

Listening to Zak's interpretation of The Who classics is like a live drum lesson. Zak seems to be the logical next step forward from Ringo, as he not only has his dad's attention to song form, tempo and musical detail, but also more drive and fire in his belly behind the kit. Zak is the genuine article as a drummer.

James McCartney

The U.K.'s *Telegraph* says of Paul McCartney's son James: "He is never likely to challenge his dad as a pop pin-up: he looks like a slightly plumper, sadder and balder ginger Paul." Beyond the remarkable facial similarity to his father, James has a similar, if thinner, vocal quality. James' first musical appearances included Paul's albums Flaming Pie (1997) and Driving Rain (2001). After his mother's death in 1998, James appeared on Linda's posthumous album Wide Prairie. Some of his youth was spent on the road with his parents and their band, Wings.

James emerged as a musician in his own right in 2009 using the name Light. Paul produced James's album *Available Light* (2010), released under James' name. His follow-up album *Close at Hand* was in stores the next year. Writers had

Paul, Linda and James McCartney

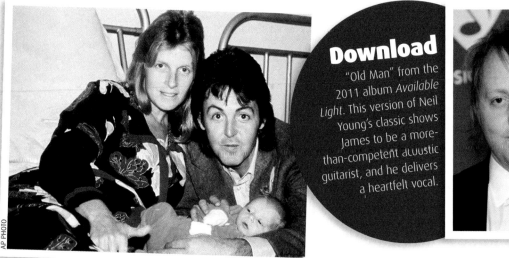

AP PHOTO

SHUTTERSTOCK / S. BUKLEY

mixed opinions about James' music. One writer said, "James has released a couple of pleasant EPs that reference sixties beat music, although more the kind of jangly rock of the Byrds and Searchers than the muscular pop of the Beatles."

James released his debut, full-length album in 2013, simply titled *Me*. Allmusic.com commented, "The melodies are direct, not elliptical, the feel is warm and enveloping — but it's the craftsmanship of *Me* that resonates, as it takes skill to create a set of songs this subtle and strong." Songs like "Wisteria" suffer some from unsure delivery and inaccurate intonation, showing James to be a hard worker musically but perhaps not gifted with a natural singing talent.

Dhani Harrison

George Harrison and second wife Olivia's only son was by his father's side during the production of his last album, Brainwashed (2001), and he sang and played guitar at the Concert for George on the first anniversary of his father's death. Dhani (pronounced Danny) earned this comment from Paul at the Concert for George: "Olivia said that with Dhani up on stage, it looks like George stayed young, and we all got old."

Dhani sings and plays lead guitar in a band he formed in 2006 called thenewno2 (pronounced "the new number two"). He says of the unusual name, which is a reference to the 1960s British television show *The Prisoner*, "I wanted it to be a faceless entity, because I didn't want to be Dhani Harrison and the Uncles, or whatever. There was just too much flak around the name Harrison at the time. I started the band so I could send anyone to a meeting, and when they were asked who they were, they could simply say 'The New No. 2.'"

You Are Here, thenewno2's debut album, was released in 2009. Allmusic.com writer Tom Forget comments, "George Harrison's son Dhani obviously has some of the biggest shoes imaginable to fill (second only maybe to poor Sean Lennon), and he's wisely decided to avoid the whole problem by following his own modern muse. The skittering beats and synths owe more to English trip-hop acts and electronic pioneers than to classic rock." Indeed, songs like "Shelter" combine electronic and rock sounds in a fresh, relaxed, inventive way, and Dhani's vocal texture is much like his father's. This is a well-rehearsed, very musical band, doing everything right, and both *Spin* and *Rolling Stone* have given the band positive reviews.

Dhani was also critical in the development of The Beatles: Rock Band game, getting Paul and Ringo's participation and striving for accuracy. Dhani said of the project, "We've been working on it for the past two years. This is the first one that is going to be totally historically accurate. It's been a real headache, but it's been the most enjoyable work I've done in my life."

In August 2010, Dhani joined with Ben Harper to form Fistful of Mercy; the band released *As I Call You Down* later that year. In 2012 thenewno2 released their second album, *thefearofmissingout*. Recently thenewno2 composed and performed the score for the film *Beautiful Creatures*. ⦾

Download

"Chose What You're Watching," a single from 2008. This is a great cut, featuring confident vocals by Dhani, hard rocking double-time drums, and catchy vocal harmonies. The bridge section has a harder edge, and the ska backbeat chorus provides an effective contrast to the earlier groove.

Mike Shellans has been on the music faculty at Arizona State University since 1985. Among his classes are Music of the Beatles and Beatles After the Beatles. His favorite Beatles' song is "Dear Prudence."

Stella McCartney

Stella McCartney

All of the Beatles's boys entered the music business, but the girls, for the most part, have steered clear of their father's profession, choosing quieter lives away from the media.

One noteworthy exception is fashion designer Stella McCartney, who is probably the best known of all the Beatles offspring. Bursting to prominence shortly after her fashion design studies were completed, Stella was named a creative director for Chloe in 1997. In 2001, she launched her own fashion house. She collaborates with Adidas on a line of sportswear and was the creative director for the British Olympic team in 2012. Like her dad, Stella balances her work with her family, and is the mother of four children.

John and
Cynthia
Lennon

John Lennon
and Yoko Ono

Jason, and daughter Lee. In January 1966, George Harrison married model Pattie Boyd, whom he had met on the set of *A Hard Day's Night* two years earlier. And, although they never married, Paul McCartney and actress Jane Asher had a well-publicized romance that lasted from 1963 to 1968. Each couple moved into its own home in the fashionable residential districts or expensive suburbs of London.

Throughout those years, news coverage of the four couples — sharing holidays, attending movie premieres, participating in the live studio broadcast of "All You Need Is Love," studying transcendental meditation in India with the Maharishi Mahesh Yogi — presented each Beatle and his partner as devoted companions, able to withstand or ignore the obvious temptations of the group's global celebrity. The women were also muses: Many of the group's most memorable songs, including Harrison's "Something" and McCartney's "And I Love Her," were inspired by their wives or girlfriends.

These relationships provided a refuge from the hectic and unpredictable life of a Beatle. As the four most famous young men on the planet — biographer Philip Norman compared them to "boy emperors and pharaohs," calling them "beings such as the modern world had never seen" — the normality and stability they found at home offered a degree of protection from the chaos, madness and adulation they encountered elsewhere.

In time, all these relationships ended. Paul and Jane parted in 1968; in the same year, John and Cynthia divorced. Ringo and Maureen divorced in 1975 and, after three years of separation, George and Pattie divorced in 1977.

Family Men BY IAN INGLIS

In the late 1960s, Timothy Leary described the Beatles as "prototypes of evolutionary agents sent by God with a mysterious power to create a new species." Their music and their deeds — the Beatles' use and advocacy of drugs, their suspicion of conventional religions, their willingness to speak out on sensitive and controversial topics, and their reassurance that all you needed was love — confirmed their position as central figures in the counterculture.

However, in one important aspect of their lives, the Beatles were profoundly conservative. The Fab Four unanimously aspired to be family men — husbands and fathers whose choices expressed continuity, not change.

Marry In Haste

John Lennon was the first to marry, in August 1962, to his pregnant girlfriend Cynthia Powell. Their son, Julian, was born the following year. In February 1965, Ringo Starr married his longtime sweetheart Maureen Cox. Within five years, they had three children — sons Zak and

Second Time Around

Rather than plunge into the carefree life of a bachelor, each of the Beatles were keen to marry again. As if seeking to replace the gap left by one partner by the speedy introduction of another, marriage followed hard on the heels of breakup. In 1969, John married Yoko Ono, and Paul married New York photographer,

George Harrison and Pattie Boyd

George and Olivia Harrison

AP PHOTO

Ringo Starr and first wife, Maureen

Ringo Starr and Barbara Bach

AP PHOTO / LAURA RAUCH

Harrison and Linda McCartney. In 2002, four years after Linda's death, Paul married Heather Mills. The couple separated in 2006 and eventually divorced in 2008. Three years later, undaunted by his experiences, Paul married Nancy Shevell: "I love being in love," he explained when asked about his enthusiasm for marriage.

Their first marriages offered a refuge from the world of the Beatles; their second marriages provided a substitute for that world. However, the most important factor in trying to understand the attractions of family life for the adult Beatles lies in the circumstances of their own childhoods. Lennon's parents separated when he was just 6 years old; he was sent to live with his Aunt Mimi. His mother, Julia, whom he saw occasionally, was killed in a traffic accident when he was 17. Ringo's parents divorced in 1943, when he was 3. At the age of 6, he spent more than a year in a hospital with peritonitis; at the age of 13, he spent another two years in a hospital with pleurisy. McCartney's mother Mary died from cancer in 1956, when Paul was 14. Only Harrison grew up in a family free from illness, divorce and early death.

Given the lack of a normal family environment in their early lives, it was hardly surprising that the Beatles were so keen to attempt to find it as adults. As youngsters who had grown up through the conflict of the 1940s and the austerity of the 1950s, they — like so many of their generation — were left to fashion an uneasy truce between the new freedoms of the 1960s and the old certainties of home and family. While being a rock star may appear to be at odds with being a family man, the Beatles desperately sought to achieve balance between the two. ○

Linda Eastman. In 1978, George married Olivia Arias. In 1981, Ringo married actress Barbara Bach.

In many ways, the Beatles' new families filled the void left by the group's demise — not just domestically, but musically. In 1970, in the sleevenotes to his first solo album, McCartney explained that his break with the Beatles was "most of all because I have a better time with my family." As if to emphasize the point, his wife Linda became a member of Wings. The McCartneys wrote, performed and toured together in Wings for the next 10 years. Their children spent time on the road with Paul and Linda.

In the same way, Yoko was an integral member of Lennon's Plastic Ono Band and an equal partner in the couple's artistic, political and musical activities. John's withdrawal from recording and performing after the birth of son, Sean, in 1975 and his pride in his new role as a househusband made it abundantly clear that the problems caused by his prolonged absences from his first family would not be repeated. And while George and Ringo's musical collaborations with the Traveling Wilburys and the All-Starr Band never included their wives, both were careful to ensure that their careers rarely took them away from their families.

Till Death Do Us Part

All of the Beatles' first marriages ended in divorce. In contrast, their second marriages continued until the premature deaths of John Lennon, George

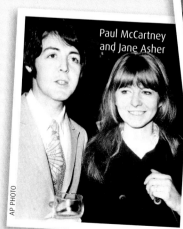

AP PHOTO

Paul McCartney and Jane Asher

AP PHOTO / PA

Paul and Linda McCartney

PRESS ASSOCIATION VIA AP IMAGES

Paul McCartney and Nancy Shevell

Across the Universe

Since their February 1964 appearance on the *Ed Sullivan Show*, the Beatles have influenced the world with more than just their music.

BY LARRY WEISMAN

They made "wooo" a lyric. They turned "yeah, yeah, yeah" into acceptable English. Meet the Beatles? I believe you're already acquainted. And of all these friends and lovers, none compare. The Beatles entered our lives and lit them up. Kids engulfed hotels that housed the Fab Four, filled arenas, appeared wild-eyed and bursting with furious passion in TV accounts of Beatles sightings. And so Beatlemania began on this side of the pond. A European madness ripped across our shores.

erse

In 1963 (opposite page) and 1964, the Beatles' popularity grew to a frenzy. Here the Fab Four wave to adoring fans after they climbed up the diving board at a Stockholm hotel pool.

In 1965,
the Beatles
showed more
maturity and
complexity in
their music,
especially with
the album
Rubber Soul.

Boys grew their hair out and walked saucily with bangs shading foreheads previously exposed by styles such as Elvis's pompadour. The tailoring of suits grew narrower as our eyes grew wider. Girls swooned, sighed and overlaid the cheeky lads from Liverpool with personalities and attributes they desired.

Beatles Domination

The Fab Four put Liverpool on the map and began the British Invasion, altering the music scene and culture forever. The Rolling Stones, The Dave Clark Five, Gerry and the Pacemakers, Peter and Gordon, Herman's Hermits, The Who, all surfed a Beatles-inspired wave that roiled the Atlantic Ocean. Rock 'n' roll, which had its roots in American rhythm and blues, bowed to the Union Jack.

The Beatles dominated radio, with 27 No. 1 hits in the U.S. and U.K., and many of those were not even their most critically acclaimed works. Meanwhile, their worldwide travels and travails made news … and television ate it up.

From modest beginnings are such events born. I sat transfixed in 1964, focused furiously on the tiny television screen in front of me, as Ed Sullivan, the preposterously stiff talent impresario who owned Sunday nights, introduced the Beatles to America before a live, screaming audience. They played, they sang, and the world changed.

Well, most of it. My father wasn't buying whatever the "mop tops" were selling, and I became a rarity in my elementary school — a kid who still had a parentally mandated crewcut. I only amplified this apparent sense of obtuseness by sticking with clarinet lessons, instead of switching, as so many of my friends did, to guitar.

I never mastered the clarinet. I ultimately learned the guitar. I will not be releasing any recordings of my performances with either instrument. But learning to play "Blackbird" on my Gibson sunburst acoustic (a 1969 model that is still in my possession) was one of my proudest moments.

Everything went Beatles. Shea Stadium, home of the New York Mets, became the site of an extraordinarily short concert in which the band found itself unable to hear its music due to the noise from the crowd. They never again played before as many as the 55,000 who packed Shea. New York went Beatles, with a disk jockey named Murray the K (Kaufman) styling himself as the Fifth Beatle. There were Beatles trading cards, pins, wigs, a cartoon series, manic and madcap movies. There were manufactured imitators who were made for TV (The Monkees) and moral opposites (the bad-boy Rolling Stones, of course).

Changing Times

As the Beatles grew and matured (they were really just teenagers when the craziness hit), their work mapped the pattern of a generation's development. Goofy, mushy teen love ("I Wanna Hold Your Hand"). A little deeper passion ("P.S. I Love You"). Introspection ("Yesterday"). The weird, vague sense that life might not be a cheery bounce free of misery and loneliness ("Eleanor Rigby"). Hazy, trippy mental gymnastics ("Within You and Without You").

They brought us the sitar and Ravi Shankar (who bequeathed us Norah Jones, bless him). They introduced us to religions and philosophies we'd never experienced when they traveled to India to study transcendental meditation with the Maharishi Mahesh Yogi. They irritated Christians worldwide with John Lennon's proclamation that the Beatles were more popular than Jesus. They preached love but sometimes, in the case of nut jobs like the murderous Charles Manson ("Helter Skelter"), they got blamed for violence. The Beatles could be whatever you thought they were, and sometimes whatever they thought they were (alternative personalities in *Sgt. Pepper's*, cartoon characters in *Yellow Submarine*).

Did we mention drugs? Mind expansion, LSD ("Lucy in the Sky with Diamonds"), other forms of substance abuse? The times practically demanded it, but the Beatles helped foment it.

The Beatles introduced in-fighting due to a celebrity marriage (Lennon and Yoko Ono). The band broke up. The Fab Four went their separate ways, got back together for a rooftop farewell concert, and again went their own ways. In a sense, they led us through our adolescence, our marriages, divorces and journeys to self-discovery. They were political (John and Yoko's Bed-In for Peace in 1969 in Amsterdam and Montreal) and anti-political (*Revolution*).

It's been 50 years since the Beatles shook those mod haircuts on American TV and set off their own revolution. Now they're scenery, background music heard in elevators, the soundtrack of our lives. The smart one, John Lennon, was shot and killed by a crazed fan in 1980. The cute one, Sir Paul McCartney, thrives in his 70s and still makes music. The quiet one, George Harrison, died of cancer in 2001. Ringo Starr, the funny one, received the French Medal of Honor in September 2013 and continues to play music and indulge a passion for photography.

Two are gone, but they, as the Beatles, endure.

Try this exercise. Ask someone to name his or her favorite Beatles' song. Now ask someone else. See how long it takes before the same song is mentioned twice.

"Michelle." "Penny Lane." "Hey Jude." "Eleanor Rigby." "Here Comes the Sun." "Something." "A Day in the Life." "Here, There and Everywhere." "Let It Be." "Ticket to Ride." The canon goes on and on. The Beatles go on and on.

As for me, I believe in "Yesterday." O

Journalist and author Larry Weisman has listened to the Beatles on vinyl, 8-track tapes, cassette tapes, CDs and via streaming audio. His favorite of the Fab Four was George Harrison.

The Fab Four donned animal costumes for their 1967 television fantasy show, "Magical Mystery Tour."

AP PHOTO

George

George Harrison

Born: Feb. 25, 1943

Died: Nov. 29, 2001
(age 58), from cancer

Marriages:
Pattie Boyd, Jan. 21, 1966-
1977 (Paul McCartney
was best man)
Olivia Trinidad Arias, Sept.
2, 1978-Nov. 29, 2001
(George's death)

Children:
Dhani Harrison, born
Aug. 1, 1978

Facts about George:

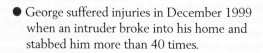

- The Harrison-written "Here Comes the Sun" is the most downloaded Beatles song on iTunes.

- George played 26 instruments, including the guitar, sitar, violin, piano, harmonica, autoharp, glockenspiel, African drum, ukulele and mandolin.

- George suffered injuries in December 1999 when an intruder broke into his home and stabbed him more than 40 times.

- George wrote "All Those Years Ago" as a tribute to John after Lennon's murder in 1980. The song featured vocal contributions from Paul and Linda McCartney and a drum part from Ringo.

- In 1978, Harrison formed HandMade Films. The most notable HandMade movies are the Monty Python films, *127 Hours* and *Lock, Stock and Two Smoking Barrels*.

- Two and a half weeks before his death, George had lunch with Paul and Ringo.

- Eric Clapton fell in love with George's first wife, Pattie Boyd, in the early 1970s and wrote "Layla" about her. Pattie eventually married Clapton in 1979 (although they divorced in 1989). Through it all, George and Clapton remained friends and jokingly called each other "husbands-in-law."